M000305741

58
SKA

Skal, David J.

Antibodies

$15.95   g /

DATE			

00760 587612

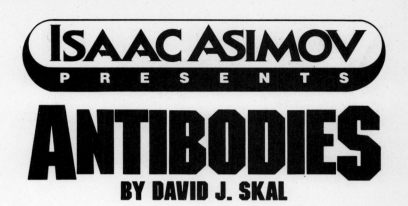

ISAAC ASIMOV PRESENTS

ANTIBODIES

BY DAVID J. SKAL

ELTING MEMORIAL LIBRARY
93 Main Street
New Paltz, New York 12561

51,646

CONGDON & WEED, INC.

New York • Chicago

In Association with Davis Publications, Inc.

Library of Congress Cataloging-in-Publication Data

Skal, David J.
  Isaac Asimov presents Antibodies.

    I. Asimov, Isaac, 1920–   II. Title.
III. Title: Antibodies.
PS3569.K36I8   1988   813'.54   87-33161
ISBN 0-86553-199-4

Copyright © 1988 by David J. Skal Associates, Inc.
International Standard Book Number: 0-86553-199-4

Published by Congdon & Weed, Inc.
A subsidiary of Contemporary Books, Inc.
298 Fifth Avenue, New York, New York 10001
Distributed by Contemporary Books, Inc.
180 North Michigan Avenue, Chicago, Illinois 60601

Published simultaneously in Canada by Beaverbooks, Ltd.
195 Allstate Parkway, Valleywood Business Park
Markham, Ontario L3R 4T8 Canada

All rights reserved
Printed in the United States of America

ELTING MEMORIAL LIBRARY
93 Main Street
New Paltz, New York 12561

COMPUTER ENVY

by Isaac Asimov

As we age, we tend to realize that the various parts of our body are wearing out. This is sad, but inevitable. If the reader happens to be young and finds this difficult to believe, all I can say is "Wait!"

We shouldn't really complain about it. Inanimate objects and even human artifacts that have no moving parts (statues, for instance) may exist, reasonably unchanged, far, far longer than we do, but anything with moving parts ages—and usually far faster than we do, but at the price of being inanimate and doing nothing.

Among living things, no mammal lives as long as human beings do, on the average, and the only animals that do better than we (turtles, for instance) are coldblooded and live quite slowly. Plants live longer still but live even more passively.

Inanimate objects with moving parts do poorly, too. A watch, or a washing machine, or an automobile that is as old as I am and has not been repaired, is not likely to be working at all.

iii

However, the point is that they can be repaired.
Little by little, you can replace this part of an automobile, then that part—the tires, the engine, the head-
lights—until no part is precisely the part that existed
when the automobile was bought and yet there will be
a continuity about it.

Why can't the body do it?

The body *does* do it, of course. Cuts and lacerations
heal, broken bones knit, and so on. The capacity for
such things decreases with age, however, and eventually the body wears out in ways that won't spontane-
ously heal, so that even if you avoid infection or accident, you die of some form of degeneration or other.

Technology comes to one's aid. Teeth decay—the
only part of the living body to do so—and that decay is
irreversible. In the old days, that meant the eventual
loss of teeth, all of them. Now metal amalgams fill the
cavities left by rot. Capping, bonding, and root canal
work make it more likely that teeth will not be lost.

I, for one, have glass lenses in front of my eyes to
supplement the natural lenses within them. In fact,
when my coronary arteries grew dangerously plugged
a few years ago, surgeons ran replacement arteries and
veins around the plugged portions (using parts of my
own arteries and veins for the purpose, to be sure) in
order to see to it that my heart continued to receive an
adequate blood supply.

Obviously, it would be nice if we could do still more.
There is the Jarvik heart which can pump away for a
while during the wait for an organic replacement to
show up. Wouldn't it be nice, though, if we had a more
permanent mechanical heart with a self-contained
energy supply that could last for centuries?

Ditto, ditto, for liver replacements, eye replacements and so on.

In fact, in my story *Bicentennial Man*, I had in the
foreground a robot that came to be more and more of a

man until he developed the final human ability of degenerative dying. In the background (I didn't make much fuss over it) were human beings who were learning to add more and more to themselves in the way of prosthetic devices in order to avoid or, at least, delay degenerative dying.

The totally unexpressed idea was that robots would become more like human beings and human beings more like robots until, finally, one couldn't tell the difference.

These ideas are not new, of course. They certainly antedate science fiction. In *Pinocchio* we have the case of a living marionette (as close to a robot as you can expect to get) who succeeds in becoming a boy, through his loyalty and bravery. For the other way around, there's *The Wizard of Oz* where a woodman who is unbelievably clumsy, accidentally mangles his various limbs with his axe and is rebuilt out of metal, so that we have the Tin Woodman, who is clearly a more permanent version of himself.

If we go back to the Greek myths, there is a trace of the mechanical replacement of parts. In one of the less pleasant myths, Tantalus, a king of Argos, was described as an intimate of the gods. Once, when he invited the gods to a banquet at his palace, he determined to test their omniscience by killing his son, Pelops, and presenting his remains as food for the banquet.

The gods realized what he had done, of course, and restored Pelops to life and arranged to have Tantalus tortured in Tartarus. There he was forced to stand in water up to his neck with delicious fruit waving before his face—but when he stooped to drink, the water level sank, and when he reached for the fruit it swayed away (hence the word "to tantalize").

However, at the banquet, the goddess Demeter, bemused by the loss of her daughter Persephone to the god of the underworld, was paying no attention and absent-mindedly ate a portion of the left shoulder of Pelops. The gods therefore replaced the missing part of the body with an ivory prosthesis—which was rather neat, I think.

But would human beings be content to have their body supplemented or even replaced by mechanical analogs? Personally, I think they would. They do not reject such things now. They do not refuse, on principle, to have their teeth filled, or to wear glasses for improving vision, or to accept replacement hip joints, or pacemakers, or artificial legs and so on.

In fact, I suspect that if these devices were markedly more efficient or longer-lasting than the "real thing," people would line up to have them. Gardner Dozois, harking back to old Sigmund Freud, calls it "computer-envy" and I think that's just the right phrase for it.

In *Antibodies*, David J. Skal takes a chilling look at the ultimate implications of just where all this may be taking us . . . and a disquieting look it is, too.

This afternoon, in bright sunlight,
I saw a young woman waiting for a
streetcar, accompanied by her body.
René Magritte

DIANDRA

She moved as if in a dream, and it was your dream, though at that point in time neither of you knew that the other existed or mattered at all.

She was a slim girl with smooth skin and wide eyes— *too wide*, people often thought—and her delicate bones pressed out against the membranes of her wrists and ankles. *Stress points*, she regarded those spots. The places of greatest mechanical wear.

She moved in front of her bathroom mirror, the dream deepening. The wide eyes remained motionless, dilated, fixed on her reflected image as she slowly rotated her head, first to the right, then to the left. The eyes held steady as gyroscopes. Unblinking. She was beyond blinking.

At last.

She had wakened early, automatically and before the alarm clock—she was superior to such things now. The changes had been slow in coming, and painful, but this morning she knew from the minute she opened her

1

eyes that her life was going to be different forever. She
was detached, now. Objective. It had been difficult, to
be sure, but she had endured the trials and now would
be rewarded. Today, when she woke just seconds before the alarm sounded—anticipating the mechanism,
eclipsing it—she knew that she had won.

She stared at her image. A taut, symmetrical face.
Long neck, hair stripped white. A strange, blue-eyed
albino. People who didn't know her associated her
look with the world of rock music, drugs. But she had
no use for these things; her image was a self-creation.
She touched her skin. It was dry, not oily, and very, very
pale. *The blood must be thinning*, she thought. Finally.

The clock radio was still playing next to the platform
on which she slept. A synthesized voice interrupted
the music every few minutes to announce the time. She
liked the voice, the chill accent of circuitry. But the
music. A silly song, about love and pain. Sillier, still,
that she let it continue. She went into the bedroom and
pulled the cord from the wall. The song continued in
her mind without distortion. What need did she have,
now, for such ridiculous props?

She surveyed the nearly unwrinkled bedclothes from
which she had risen. Another test. And on the chrome
bedstand was her reward. The envelope containing the
one-way airline ticket that, today, would allow her to
break utterly with the past.

*. . . unfortunately, the procedures are still consid-
ered "illegal" in this country . . . but a limited number
of the most deserving among you may be accepted
into certain Central American clinics. . . .*

And Diandra was among the most deserving.

She drifted out into her apartment, ignoring the
kitchen. Withdrawing from food had been the most
difficult test, but she had faith in her teachers, and
gradually the pangs subsided. The appliances—the refrigerator, the stove, the food processor—were all

beautiful objects in themselves. Cool surfaces and lines, stainless steel and glass, a pristine laboratory devoid of organic matter.

Beyond the kitchen was the living room, the room where she spent most of her time. It had served as a kind of cocoon, this room . . . a suspended grid of track lighting, industrial carpeting, high-tech chrome and wire and glass. One wall was dominated by a poster graphic by H. R. Giger, a surrealistic fusion of machine and man. The effect was at once futuristic and ancient, the anticipation of a forgotten revelation. Beneath the graphic was a videocassette player and its symbiotic screen . . . how much she had learned from *this* machine! Stacked nearby were the *Lectures from the Cybernetic Temple*, which she knew by heart, and other cassettes of motion pictures with titles like *Alien*, *Robocop*, and *Tron*. The room was also littered with electronic game cartridges, science fiction magazines, and medical journals.

All vestiges of a former life. A life she had outgrown. She would go to work as usual, arouse no suspicions. There were enemies everywhere, watching. It was important to go through the motions.

She dressed in a crisp black jumpsuit that dramatically complemented her hair. She tied it with a silver corded belt. Then she picked up the airline ticket, examined it along with her passport, and slipped them both into the brightly dyed gas mask bag she used for a purse. She packed no other luggage. She didn't need any. Where she was going, everything would be taken care of. For once and for all.

As she left the Pacific Avenue apartment, the three-and-a-half rooms that had housed her in this year of transformation, she felt no regret, no loss, only liberation. Her landlady, Minnie, said hello in the hallway, but Diandra pretended not to hear. Minnie, who had slipped magazine articles under her door. Articles that dealt with anorexia nervosa, an affliction the landlady evidently believed had invaded her premises. Minnie, so physically decrepit herself, so near death—was that where her interest in Diandra's body derived? Anorexia nervosa! No, Diandra was not anorexic. It was true she didn't eat, had slimmed herself to a sliver . . . but anorexia? How typical of Minnie to see the world in tabloid headlines. How typical and how blind.

"Diandra!" the old woman cried. "If you have time, I thought I could make you some breakfast—"

Diandra looked back up the stairs. She looked at Minnie and did not speak.

"—you young people are so *frantic*, always rushing about, you don't take the time to *nourish* yourselves properly."

"Thank you, Minnie. But I'm fine."

"I know you think I'm a busybody, prying into your eating habits—"

"You really won't have to worry about that. Not anymore. I'm taking care of everything. Really."

"I'm glad, but . . . you still look so wan! I worry about you. I worry about *all* the young people in the building."

"Yes, Minnie. Thank you. Good-bye."

Yes. Good-bye.

Outside, the morning fog was burning off. Diandra could just discern the TransAmerica pyramid jutting through the scudding mist. She liked the building, defiant against the skyline, and identified with its hard-edged solitude. Like a big mechanical fang, she thought, taking a bite of the sky.

She rode the Van Ness-Sutter bus; smooth, quiet, and electric. The other passengers didn't bother her much today; she was beyond all that now. Beyond noticing, as she usually did, the broken-down, flabby bodies; the pungency of the flesh masked by colognes and preparations. Today her eyes scanned over and past them. She was interested only in the reality of the machine in which they traveled, the surrounding machines and machine-made structures. The only lasting reality.

Not bodies. Not flesh.

The bus lurched and came to a stop at Union Square. She rose from her seat automatically, moved efficiently past the bodies that didn't really matter, not now, and alighted on the sidewalk outside the imposing Art Deco department store that was her destination. *Croesus*. A San Francisco institution, the store was built in the early 1930s, a nervous amalgam of the machine aesthetic tempered with Spanish affectation—now a hybrid architectural classic. A special nonprofit organization had been formed in the late seventies to save it from the wrecker's ball and succeeded in having it declared a historic landmark.

Diandra entered, as she had always entered, through revolving doors set in glass brick and surrounded by chrome filigree. The main floor was a delirious blend of perfumes and Aztec columns. Every day for the last year Diandra had passed through these doors, was spun through them literally, and every day she passed among the oddly metallic scents that soothed and excited her simultaneously. The store's interior was silver and spotless. Everything was so wonderfully controlled, so meticulously engineered. She rode the escalator to the mezzanine, past chunky silver lightning bolts and toward a ceiling that seemed to descend like a hydraulic press. On either side she watched other banks of escalators where people moved peacefully, automatically from level to brightly lit level and where, on the top floor, Diandra imagined the light would be beatific and blinding, with customers kneeling to receive the Croesus charge plate on their tongues.

. . . think of yourselves as pioneers, explorers venturing into uncharted lands that will forever alter the course of human destiny! Many of you have felt iso-

lated in your present lives, alienated in some way from the world around you. But of course! You are different. You are special. And now the time has come for your natural superiority to be recognized. . . .

She punched the time clock in the drab workers' station just off the mezzanine. This part of the building had not been extended the "landmark" treatment, although a few pieces of ratty Art Deco furniture had been thrown into service as an "employees' lounge." A young floorwalker from appliances sat on the edge of a pie-shaped divan, trembling as she sipped coffee from a Styrofoam cup. The girl was homely, nearly obese. She stared at Diandra over the rim of the cup. The girl had often watched her in these silent moments of morning intersection, watched her with a peculiar hungry intensity. What did she want? She had never spoken. Only watched.

Diandra went into the staff locker room and checked the message board for the last time. Never again. That done, she went into the lavatory, not to use one of the stalls—the idea was ridiculous now—but instead to gaze again into the mirror, to make sure nothing had changed, that the image was fixed as before. Yes . . . the exquisitely balanced head, poised in perfect alignment . . .

There was someone behind her.

She turned. And cursed the burst of adrenaline inside her. She wasn't supposed to *feel*—

Standing inside the lavatory door was the girl from the lounge. Her skin looked pasty in the fluorescent light. There was nothing furtive about her gaze now. But if her stare was direct, it was not without a crazy touch of fear.

"What do you want?" Diandra asked, controlling herself.

"I've . . . I've never talked to you before," the girl began, and Diandra turned away. What did this creature want? Did it have to be *today*? She clutched the sink and tried not to look at the fat girl's reflection over the basin.

"I . . . I know what you are," the girl stammered. Did she have a name? Diandra didn't know. "I know because I'm *like* you. I'm . . . I'm like you, and I don't know what to do—" Her voice rose sharply. Her body quivered. "I want you to help me."

"I really don't know what I can—" She had to get out of here. Perhaps somebody else would come in.

The girl drew closer. "I've watched all the tapes, read the books, but I don't know where to go. *You* have the connections—you can't lie to me!" Her voice grew breathy and she moved toward the sink, toward Diandra and her secrets.

"Look," she said, her voice a whisper, "I had this done in Nevada." She held out a bandaged hand and ceremoniously unwrapped the dressing from the little finger. But from the first knuckle outward there was no finger at all, just a tiny, light-emitting diode in the shape of a human digit. The base of the graft was raw and infected. Diandra stared, transfixed. The prosthesis pulsed out light in a domino pattern where the fingernail would have been. "I went to this clinic in the desert—I paid them a thousand dollars, and they just disappeared. I woke up like *this*, and they were gone— I even found my finger in a sink . . ."

There were tears in her eyes, and Diandra was terrified the girl would try to embrace her.

"It was supposed to be the first step, a sacrament; I heard all about it. The Cybernetic Temple. But now the graft isn't taking, and I don't know what to do—"

Diandra pulled away from the sink. She flattened against the wall next to a tampon dispenser and did not move. The girl's tears were copious now. "I know . . . I *know* what you're thinking . . . that I'm disgusting, I'm fat . . . but do you think I like it any better? I just want a way out—"

Only a limited number will be chosen.

"You reach out for help . . . they cut off your hand—"

"I really have to leave," said Diandra, steadying herself. Her internal gyroscope was threatening to fail her. The girl blocked the lavatory door. Diandra could smell her now, a meaty smell, a smell of panic, and because she could smell her she was part of her . . .

The girl continued, relentless. "I know now that this country's good for nothing, you've got to go *outside* to get what you want—"

"You're very upset—"

"—and don't tell me you don't know where to go! I saw you go to the airline counter last week . . . I followed you at lunchtime—"

"I'm not going anywhere. I just want to leave—"

"Don't you understand? I *want* them to cut away the rest. All the fat! All the past! All the everything! I want to be a perfect little robot just like you're going to be . . . a *robot*, yes, don't tell me that isn't what you have in mind."

Diandra felt herself sliding toward a raw, animal panic. This bloated creature was dragging her down, dragging her back. *The poisonous secretions of the flesh are a constant, contagious enemy of the mind. Declare yourself in opposition to them now! The body will destroy you; only the Temple will set you free.*

"Meat!" said Diandra, with a venom that surprised her.

"Wha—?"

"You were *born* meat and you will *die* meat! I can do nothing for you!" She poked at the fat girl. She went reeling toward a stall. She gasped, slipped. Diandra felt her control returning. "One of *us*? Just look at you!" She felt her voice to be a sibilant, hissing current emitted from a loudspeaker at the center of her being.

"—nothing but a bag of maggots! How *dare* you approach one of my kind, how *dare* you even come near—"

The girl's face shivered like gelatin. But then an angry storm cloud seemed to throw its shadow across her features. "You're not so much!" she spat. "What happened to me can happen to you. *Parts* wear out. *Things* fall apart. And . . ." she giggled maliciously, raising one hand to her mouth. ". . . there are always *gremlins* that get into machinery."

"You're insane," Diandra said, almost under her breath. Was she insane, too?

"You act so superior. But you're not one of them *yet*, you skinny bitch! When they cut you, you'll bleed, just like me. You want to see?"

Diandra did not want to see. She gasped as the girl's arm shot toward her. But the hand held no knife; instead she pulled back her sleeve to reveal the vertical scars on her wrist. Ragged, puckered, colored like worms. She had already done cutting of her own. Much of it.

Diandra fled the lavatory. She couldn't have been more shaken had the girl actually opened a vein and sprayed her with blood. *A madwoman trapped inside her body. Screaming in a toilet, with a winking electric finger. Screaming for release.*

Dizzy, that part of her being she had come to think of as *the gyroscope* failing her, she took the service elevator to the display department. She was shaking almost uncontrollably . . . the *body* was shaking her. She couldn't let anyone see her like this; not anyone in the store, nor later on the plane, and especially, *especially* not the bodiless voices of the Cybernetic Temple, voices she had been chosen to meet directly, whose emissaries would greet her on a tropical airstrip in a place called Boca Verde.

No. Resist. Appearances were important. *Achieve the semblance. The reality will follow.*

The Art Deco floor indicator completed its arc like the flourish of a baton. She had only partially regained her composure when the elevator door slid open and Philip, her supervisor, caught sight of her.

"Diandra . . . is anything wrong?" Philip was a smooth, elegantly entertaining man she had met at a party in New York. She and Philip had been attracted to each other immediately, on a level that had nothing whatsoever to do with *bodies*. The realization excited her: she could live in San Francisco and never have to deal with men *that* way. They didn't seem to realize that she enjoyed them not for what they were but for what they were not. Philip's interest was primarily professional. He had admired her portfolio of fashion magazine graphics—unusually hard-edged, cubistic, and surreal—and had intuited, correctly, that her abilities could be translated effectively to the art of three-dimensional display. Under his tutelage, she had blossomed as a window dresser and more—an environmental designer whose concepts were setting new standards for visual marketing. And putting Croesus back on the map.

But lately, her mind seemed elsewhere.

"I'm fine, Philip. Really."

Philip stared at her, his left eyebrow tossed above the rim of the ruby-rimmed aviator glasses he affected but did not require.

"Really?" he asked. "Because I find it very difficult to believe that somebody who feels so fine can look like such shit."

"Philip, I'm really not in the mood—" She brushed past him. The fat girl in the lavatory—how much did she know about Boca Verde? Did others know, too?

"Not in the mood, I know. You haven't been in the mood for much of anything for quite some time now. I'm still waiting for the revised sketches on the fifth floor installation, and I expect them today. I don't care how much press you've gotten lately, this is still *my* department—"

"Yes, Philip—"

"—and whatever has been bothering you I want you to leave on the street level and not drag it up here. Is it that Cybernetic Temple nonsense?"

"It's not the Temple. You don't understand the Temple."

"I suppose I don't. And from what little you told me I don't want to understand it. Starving yourself, reading all that science fiction crap—"

"You like 'that science fiction crap' well enough when I put it on the display floor. The fifth floor installation, for example."

"Touché, Diandra."

"Look. I'm sorry I'm late. I've been under a lot of pressure. It won't happen again." Of course it wouldn't happen again. She wouldn't be here for it to happen again. There had been a time when she thought Philip might be able to share her excitement about the Temple and what it promised for her. But even he grew alienated by the Temple's precepts. After that, she resolved never to trust anyone but the Voices. *No doubt the people around you will notice changes in your behavior. You must become skillful at deflecting them by whatever means possible. Resistance to the Temple is intense! Do not encourage it!*

"Diandra. I want you to take care of yourself. Not just because of what you're doing for the store, but because we're friends. Or were friends, once."

"I'm . . . changing, Philip. It's nothing personal."

"Of course you're changing. You've gone farther more quickly than I would ever have predicted. And I suppose you'll go your own way soon. But *please* let's have a little more structure in this department. I'm also under a lot of pressure, you know. From upstairs."

"All right, Philip. I'll try." Boca Verde. Boca Verde. Boca Verde—

Diandra forced a smile. Philip seemed satisfied, at least for the time being. That was all that mattered. The time being. Just for the rest of the day . . .

Alone in her studio, a cold, crazy sweat spread under her jumpsuit. Was she melting down, falling apart? Had she forgotten everything she had learned? She had to regain control. Control was everything. Somehow that creature in the toilet had contaminated her, shaken her faith. *You're not one of them yet.*

No. Not yet. But soon. She would find the strength, would do her silly little job, and then she would leave. Take her passport and go to the airport and say good-bye to this "life" forever. It was Friday. It would be days before anyone started to look for her.

If she could just get through the day.

Automatically, she moved to the mannequin locker and wheeled out her favorite. She had designed it personally, a prototype for fashion experiments, never for public display. Diandra saw the mannequin as an idealized version of herself. And she named her Dionne.

Dionne was more than a mannequin. She was a sophisticated machine, an instrument upon which Diandra played the most *outré* fantasies of fashion. The android look was the latest rage. The more nonhuman the window and floor displays became, the more the public was excited. And the more excited the public became, the more they came to Croesus and the more they bought. They bought fantasies of tranked-out women with glowing optical fibers for hair and video beam projectors for eyes. They craved high-tech tableaux of robotresses deflecting laser pulses off provocative Mylar lingerie. Mechanical women with portable color televisions in place of heads. It was Diandra who dreamed these dreams . . . Diandra, with Dionne.

Dionne stood motionless, a bald, gleaming statue with supple latex skin stretched tight over a fully jointed skeleton. Even her fingers could be manipulated; they snapped into place with a satisfying pop. The breasts were filled with a thick liquid polymer that conformed perfectly to the shape of any garment she wore. Diandra turned the head toward her and pressed the temples with her thumb. The standard eyes tumbled into her other, waiting hand. She replaced them with iridescent pinballs . . . an especially futuristic effect was called for today. Perhaps that new, aluminized fabric that fell in such interesting folds. She took the fabric from its shelf. It seemed to whisper as she pulled it toward her, a sibilant sound: *yes, yes*.

She pulled down a length of photographic backdrop paper from its overhead roll and activated a slide projector. She had collected numerous images of tropical jungles. The slide label said *Henri Rousseau: The Jesters*. But to Diandra, it was *Boca Verde*. The most restful image she knew.

And yet—

—mindbody meatbody deathbody stinking sagging shitting fetus bursting organs hanging buried alive in a coffin of blood oh god not me don't let it be me got to get out of this bucket of tripe it's sucking me down throwing me up take it away this pulsing writhing spurting spinning body-go-round, body-go-round, BODY—

The vision—so sudden, so visceral, so vividly hallucinatory—acted on her like an electrical shock. Her heart pounded. *Body*. Her limbs trembled. *Body*. Nausea curled in her gut like a demanding child. She was losing. The plane ticket, the promises, Boca Verde— they were all a joke. Unless . . .

Dionne stared through her, past her. Cool, mechanical, self-contained. *Complete*.

Diandra anchored the legs to a pedestal, spread the arms in a welcoming gesture. The pinball eyes reflected her own image, diminished in convexity. The Rousseau jungle rippled and came alive with the movement of the hanging paper. *Boca Verde*. Yes, she was almost there. Diandra took the glimmering fabric and joined Dionne on her pedestal. She shook out the cloth and gathered it in large, silvery swags. She wrapped it around Dionne's cool waist. One line suggested itself, then another . . . over one shoulder and around . . . pliable breasts hammocked in silver. She wrapped herself in the fabric as well, conjoining herself to her creation. She let herself fall limp against the android. It was good. It was a cocoon. Dionne would watch over her. She would be very still and very quiet, she would hardly even breathe . . . that was all that was needed . . .

And Boca Verde, the green mouth, swallowed her whole.

She did not hear Philip when he came back, and at first he did not see her, so preoccupied was he with another image.

". . . terrible, Diandra, terrible, a girl from appliances just killed herself, she forced open an elevator shaft and—Diandra? What is this . . . some kind of joke? *Oh my God . . . Diandra! Is everyone here going crazy?*"

JULIAN

An American ritual begins.

Technicians check light levels. Sullen, requisite union personnel shift their weight just enough to make their presence known. But it is your presence that is important today . . . you have often taken part in these rites, are adept at them. You command a certain amount of respect; you have won it in repeated talk-show clashes. For no matter how much you might anger a host, no matter how you might break the rules, the media will always be interested in your work. The ratings demand it. For your name is synonymous with topics that the producers cannot ignore. Cults . . . behavior modification . . . brainwashing . . . sex in all its possible manifestations. Your alleged work with "illicit" drugs (toxins, the press has gone so far as to call them) . . . religion-versus-state controversies . . .

You may be the ultimate talk-show guest.

A closed-circuit television monitor radiates your image in monotonous Warhol-style . . . the motionless,

15

automatic camera registers you unblinkingly. You have ideal television features, better than those of the hostess who will grill you (on some unconscious level she realizes this, and it will fuel her antagonism). In real life your features are not remarkable save for their sharpness . . . in "real life" people sometimes think you have a pinched or priggish look. But on low-resolution television your profile cuts the interference like a snow melter. Even in the worst reception areas your high cheekbones and deep-set eyes lose little of their definition . . . network anchormen would pay a plastic surgeon handsomely to re-create your physiognomy. "Hawklike," some said. "Hatchetlike," said another. Your eyebrows were "dramatic." They were fused, knitted. In fact they were your most dramatic feature, a solid accent bar straight across your brow. It is a good face, and a good *television* face, if only because it can be translated into sharp-edged planes of light and shadow, reduced to a cartoon and still be recognizable as human. As *you*.

Your relationship with the media has always been stormy, ambivalent. You create for them the kind of controversy on which they thrive, and still they try to tear you down. You know all the tricks. The sound engineers who try to intimidate you by asking you to attach your own microphone, rudely ask you to speak louder, create crashing disturbances offscreen to catch you off guard and make you look ridiculous. They have tried everything. Everything. They love their machines, their tubes and wires, they are so much like the creatures you crusade against—perhaps this is why they struggle so to defeat you.

The talk-show hostess arrives, her eyes popping with their tinted plastic lenses, her auburn hair shellacked into a rigid nimbus. She holds a clipboard, talks sharply to her underlings. She is dressed in a blue tailored suit, is heavily made up . . . everyone else in the room is dressed in grubby work clothes. Only you and she stand out. She avoids your gaze completely as you sit in the leatherette swivel chair on the carpeted platform. Behind you are cardboard cutouts, starburst patterns (or are they daisies?) six feet high. All so incredibly cheap and tacky close up . . . and yet, on-screen they convey a living room ambience, warmth, bonhomie. The talk-show hostess strides back and forth . . . she seems electrified, overly animated. Yes, she is determined to avoid any direct contact with you before the taping . . . she has dealt with you already through intermediaries, research assistants, perhaps even watched you on videotape in a similar "interview" situation. Even during the interview, her eyes will be fixed on a monitor above your shoulder, not on you.

It is going to be a difficult interview. But you are prepared. You have fallen into their traps before.

"Good morning, everyone. I'm Leah Lavin, and welcoming you to 'Fault Lines,' San Francisco's morning talk show that points fingers, names names . . . and sometimes just has a little fun. This morning we'll be covering the growing menace of poisons in the home — not the kind under the sink, but chemical threats that may be posing health hazards for your family without your even knowing it. Sounds scary? You bet. We'll also be hearing a little later about sexual abuse of senior citizens in an Oakland nursing home and then switch live to 'Fault Lines' 's 'no-fault' chef, Ramon, live at Fisherman's Wharf, where he'll be showing you how to create a 'no-fault' cioppino of your own—

"But first, I'll introduce you to a man who has been called 'The Rod Serling of Psychotherapy' and who has brought to light a truly chilling twilight zone of mental disorder and who has stirred up a lot of people in the process. His methods are a little unorthodox, and he'll be with us to answer some hard questions right after this message."

A brief reprise of the opening computer animation, then a slam cut to a florid Daly City salesman of home computers. He attacks his job with the energy of a used-car dealer in the thick of a price war. Your eyes are on Leah, however. She still hasn't looked at you and is consulting fretfully with her hair stylist and an associate producer. Her manner is almost like that of a boxer in the ring—you almost expect someone to hand her a flask.

You like your women fearful, fretful, animated just to the verge of panic. They're easy to handle. Predictable. And so, so deluded if they think they're going to get the better of you on a television talk show.

Out of camera view, your penis surges, filling out a damp pocket of space between your trouser leg and thigh. A throbbing metronome for the exercise that will follow. You swivel the chair in Leah's direction. You do not wear underwear—it is so unnatural, confining!—and so the shaft is clearly defined. Leah notices—suddenly—and her face registers an amalgam of fascination and disgust that excites you all the more.

You are not one to make a secret of your biological urges.

No one is actually watching you except Leah. The technicians, the associate producers, all are intent on the television monitors. No one but Leah can see what is happening—below the waist, you do not exist. Your erection grows bolder. Quietly, you unzip. The audience will see nothing.

Just before the interview begins, Leah looks at you briefly—from the shoulders up—and something like a smile cracks a fissure in her makeup. But a red light distracts her, and she turns just in time to light up the living rooms of a quarter million housewives.

"Our first guest this morning is perhaps one of the most controversial figures in the Bay Area, if not the country. Dr. Julian Nagy, executive director and founder of Marin County's Resurrection House, has been making headlines for the past year because of his work treating members of certain cults—"

"There is only *one* cult I am concerned with—"

"—and who has been accused of operating a cult of his own in the process. Resurrection House focuses its attention on 'antibodies' or 'robopaths'—men and women who believe—*really* believe—that they are more like machines than human beings and whose numbers have been proliferating at an alarming rate. Dr. Nagy, I believe you view the syndrome as an understandable, if extreme, reaction to the technological society in which we live?"

"On one level, yes. The machine, whatever else it is, is one of the twentieth century's prime symbols of alienation and dehumanization. So, it's not unusual to find alienated human beings coming to terms with the machine by identifying with it. But what is unusual is the shocking *extremes* to which the antibodies have taken this identification. Not only do they identify with machines; they actively seek and expect to *become* machines. Like transsexuals who feel trapped in the body of the opposite sex, and seek surgical release, the antibody cannot abide having a body at all. We're dealing with extremely suggestible individuals here, who fall prey to both their own delusions and the manipulations of others."

"By manipulations, you mean—"

You show her what you mean. You take out your cock and aim it like a gun. Your voice betrays nothing.

"I mean *direct* exploitation by both self-proclaimed messiahs and even elements of organized crime. An antibody has no allegiance to the 'biological' world, and, like the hardcore drug addict, is capable of the most violent and antisocial behavior imaginable. Especially if he has been promised the reward of an artificial body part or some other radical procedure."

"But surely, they don't actually—" Disbelieving, she stares at your lap.

"Miss Lavin, at this very minute there are former American citizens who are undergoing the most terrifying kinds of surgical experimentation, the kind of thing that hasn't been seen since Nazi Germany. Most of it is being carried out in South American clinics, and with the full cooperation of the victims. Our own intelligence agencies have documentation of what is going on, despite the public silence, and Resurrection House has filed a class action suit for full disclosure of our government's knowledge and support of these activities."

"Many people call your accusations wild, even inflammatory. And they also say that your own organization is itself not much more than a sadistic concentration camp, in which patients are subjected to incredible degradation and filthy living conditions—"

"It's very easy to take my work out of context, to focus on the sensational aspects. But, of course! My treatment *is* sensational, by definition, *concerned* with the senses, the body and its perceptions. Resurrection House provides a form of somatic shock therapy—the only effective technique for repairing the ruptured connection with the reality of the organism."

"It's been said you keep your patients in pens, unwashed—"

"America's morbid obsession with antisepsis has done its share to create this problem. So, yes, many of the so-called 'hygienic' rituals of modern life are dispensed with as part of the deprogramming process. You must remember that Cybernetic Temple members are living in a kind of hypnotic trance, the victims of a deep and insidious form of brainwashing. As far as I can tell, Resurrection House methods have been the only effective ones in breaking through to these people. Can you dispute this?"

You toss off the challenge with a disarming smile. She

ignores it and continues with her prepared questions.

"What about this temple? Where is it located? Why can't it be stopped?"

"No one knows where it is. It seems to 'exist' only on videocassettes that its members circulate among themselves. The tapes are incredibly sophisticated, at least the ones we have analyzed—not only do they include visual and audio propaganda, but layer upon layer of subliminal cues and instructions. Even the most wary viewer can't help being affected. Where these things are being manufactured and just who is behind it simply isn't known. But whoever it is knows exactly what they're doing and they have the money to do it. And as I mentioned before, the authorities are simply not doing their part to investigate these things—"

"Aren't you perhaps overreacting? San Francisco has always been a place where unorthodox cults and movements have gotten started. Won't this Cybernetic Temple just run its course and fade away like so many other fads?"

"Miss Lavin, I certainly hope you don't consider brainwashing, human vivisection, and incitement to terrorism a 'fad'—"

"I didn't mean—"

"Well, I hope you didn't. Someone—some megalomaniac oil tycoon, some perverted multinational corporation, some foreign power, perhaps even a covert intelligence agency of our own government—is experimenting at this very moment with the most potent and destructive form of behavior control ever invented, turning Americans by the tens of thousands into literal guinea pigs. Resurrection House may be the only place in America that offers any protection—"

"Resurrection House—where does the name come from?"

"Why, from 'the resurrection of the body,' of course."

Release.

"Of course. And on that messianic note, we will leave Dr. Julian Nagy for this word from our sponsor . . ."

"You pig," the talk show hostess snarls. "You filthy pig. In all my life I've *never*—" She struggles to disengage herself from the microphone umbilicus that ties her to the set, to you. Your erection is subsiding, the dark wet stain on your leg spreading onto the padded swivel chair. You have achieved another milestone in your life—you have brought yourself to orgasm live on daytime television. You make no effort to cover the results. Someone will have to wipe the runny semen from the chair before the next guest, you suppose. Perhaps they will replace the chair. Probably.

"Robert—help me with this microphone!" She is trapped. As her flunky extricates her from her technological snare, she continues: "I'll see that you never get booked on this station again. If it's the last thing I do—"

"If you try, it *will* be the last thing you do. At least at this station." And you are right. You have the ratings to prove it.

You deftly remove your microphone, retrieve your raincoat, and leave the set. The entire staff stands frozen, watching you. The stain glistens. You are still in the spotlight. You will always be in the spotlight. You must. You.

•

But even as you have won this little encounter, another is being prepared. Ambulances converge on a department store off Union Square. A crowd gathers. Two inert forms are carted out. One is for the morgue—your dream was too much for her. The other . . . she is for you. Covered in a shroud of silver lamé, clutching an airline ticket. She is rigid, motionless, a machine deprived of power. The crowd surges forward. *Such a striking girl—what's wrong with her . . . ?* Her *rigor vivus*-in-life excites them as it will excite you. As for the shapeless thing in the body bag—well, what is real death compared to this thrilling facsimile? The ambulance door closes. The process has begun that will soon deliver Diandra unto you . . . *Diandra*, a name you have never heard, or dreamed of, though Diandra herself is very much a part of your dream.

Whether you are a part of hers will have to be determined.

GILLIAN

As Gillian sat in her Mill Valley breakfast room of wicker and rattan, sipping her third cup of French espresso while her husband consummated an auto-erotic fantasy live on a television talk show, she almost thought: the bastard has nerve. Almost, for time and futility had succeeded in discouraging such wasteful expenditures of energy. It would lead inevitably to frustration, like the time a hurricane had been given her name, only to be downgraded to a tropical depression before it could do any damage.

Her marriage, she realized, had become one long exercise in resource conservation. Sometimes she thought she was running the Sierra Club.

She sipped her espresso, laced liberally with cinnamon, and tried to determine the exact moment of her husband's out-of-frame orgasm. He was a sneaky devil, but she could tell from his expression that he was ready to pop . . . he had done something similar at a recent dinner party in Pacific Heights. At first she

thought it might all have to do with the male meno-
pause, but soon she could see it as part of a larger
pattern of changes that had been overtaking Julian
since their move from Connecticut eight years earlier.

The druggy, sex-charged atmosphere of their new
environment had almost immediate shaping effects on
the New England behavior modification specialist (Gillian couldn't believe her ears when she first heard him,
at a Sausalito reception, refer to his work as "behavior
mod." But that was just the beginning.) Julian began
using fewer and fewer of his shirt buttons, was fitted
with gas-permeable contact lenses. He was changing,
and he was obsessed with the need to change others as
well.

After a trial separation and reconciliation (Julian was
difficult even in Connecticut), they had come to San
Francisco in order that Julian could assume the co-
directorship of a fashionable weight-reduction clinic
in Marin County. At the time, he was not completely
aware of the clinic's financial mismanagement. As a
result, the organization nearly defaulted on several
capital loans, the other co-director abandoned ship,
and Julian was left with the bag and a number of tax
lawyers. After a nerve-racking year, the clinic was reor-
ganized as a tax-exempt foundation with a new focus:
the deprogramming and rehabilitation of victims of
pseudo-religious cults that Julian correctly predicted
would become a major growth industry in the Bay
Area.

Gillian couldn't help but notice her husband's attraction to the pliable young female cultists . . . on the
surface they were so innocent, so natural. So willing to
be used. Gillian was startled at first, then hurt when
she realized the intensity of excitement these brainwashed bimbos elicited in him. He always told his wife
that it was her stubbornness, her willful intellectual
edge, that he found exciting. Sexual attraction was

based on a certain amount of resistance, wasn't it? But Gillian knew that the level of excitement she was witnessing in her husband far surpassed anything she had been able to coax from him in their years of marriage. The Cybernetic Temple, with its ripe herd of mechanical sheep, tapped in her husband a lustful wellspring of unimaginable depth. He talked excitedly about restoring these people to their bodies, or at least to an awareness of them. But what really turned him on was the prospect of using his own body in the process. These young California cultists—men as well as women, she was almost certain of that—were almost impossibly insulated from sensation, autistic virgins who, by offering the greatest amount of resistance, afforded the most intense pleasure.

They didn't talk much about what pleasured him; there was an unspoken understanding between them that Gillian had always been, well, inadequate somehow. It was one way he had of controlling the relationship: never being satisfied, always having the power of approval. As if to say, *all things considered, you're damn lucky I'm still holding on to you.*

Damned, yes. Lucky, no.

And still she kept coming back to him.

At least until now.

Gillian rose from the rattan chaise, went to the island kitchen, and rinsed out her mug. This game between Julian and herself was wearing thin. Too thin. She had become testier with him than usual, especially on the subject of his psychotic clientele.

"Why make such a big thing out of it?" she had asked him. "Why not *let* them be machines if that's what they want? How can you stop it? Ban all the pocket calculators so somebody won't OD?"

"Are you trying to be flippant, Gillian? I take my work seriously, you know."

"If what you're saying about this cult is true,

somebody better have a sense of humor about it."

"That's right, Gillian. Laugh it off. Toss it off like one of your glib magazine pieces. At this very moment there may be a conspiracy among the highest levels of corporate finance and government intelligence to turn people into computer components, and you want to make jokes. Maybe you could write a cute feature about it for one of these illiterate California newspapers."

The crack about her writing hurt. Julian had never taken her literary aspirations seriously . . . possibly because she had never taken them seriously herself. In Connecticut she had begun several "serious" novels, one about existentialism and bag ladies, another about cancer, and still another about layers of illusion in a New England summer stock theatre. But no matter where she hid them, Julian found the manuscripts, read them, and made fun of them. Nothing vicious, just enough to deflate her commitment to fiction and keep her grinding out "lifestyle" schlock for the Sunday Connecticut section of *The New York Times*. She still read the Sunday *Times* faithfully, satellite-sent at $3.50 a throw.

But the storyteller inside would not shut up. A few years after relocating to California, and after once more establishing herself as a dependable stringer of insipid "lifestyle" features to regional magazines, she could take no more. As a private indulgence, she began to write a novel lampooning Julian's new endeavors. She found the whole "antibody" phenomenon to verge on the ludicrous. It was all so materialistic, so gadget-oriented, so predictably American. And yet it was interesting. Damned interesting. People turning into machines . . . there could be a market for this. She spent a few weeks reading formula science fiction paperbacks to get the feel of the terrain. Then she let it rip, writing two thousand words a day in longhand on yellow legal pads she bought by the dozen in San Rafael.

When it was finished, she called her old agent in New York, swearing her to secrecy about the entire project. If published, the novel would have to appear pseudonymously. The byline Gillian chose was "A. R. Delamarvia."

The title of the book was *Helen Keller in Outer Space*.

Three months after she submitted the manuscript to her agent, she had a sale. Her agent, Cherie, placed prepublication excerpts in strategic magazines (like the women's science fiction glossy, *Cassiopeia* and *Otherlips*, a feminist review). By the time the paperback hit the stands, an audience was ready and waiting. A year later, *Helen Keller in Outer Space* was an underground best-seller.

> From the dark side of the moon, Lara looked up at the big blue marble she had fought so long to escape. It appeared so serene, now, so peaceful and unthreatening. But Lara knew the truth. She was a telepath, an ultra-sensitive receptor to whom even the most civilized of Terran cities was a psychic hell. Every waking and sleeping moment her mind had been filled with the background noise of human suffering. The sensitivity had developed slowly at first, and then with increasing speed until her awareness was like a radio frequency jammed by choruses of the damned. Earlier she had been a trailblazer in the field of parapsychiatry, an extraordinary diagnostician as a result of her gift. But at the end she had been reduced to an exposed nerve, herself near-psychotic. This prototype moonbase for medical research was the only possible refuge for her, a quarter million miles from the angst of civilization.

While Gillian's heroine had achieved legendary status on Earth, there were, of course, those who enjoyed her exile. One of these was Dr. Zyglos, moonbase chief of medicine, a misogynist who gloated over the fate of this woman who had gone too far, achieved too much. In the course of the novel Zyglos, with oily condescension and smirking politeness, treats her like a quasi-patient, although she is in reality a fellow researcher. The fact that Lara can read his mind makes things all the worse.

The "Helen Keller" angle of the story derives from Lara's attempt to communicate telepathically with a catatonic enemy "mindship," believed to harbor valuable military intelligence.

> ". . . a mindship?"
> "Exactly what it sounds like," said Zyglos. "A surveillance craft piloted by a human brain grafted into a computer. They raise them that way from birth, to hate their bodies. At age ten they have a big ceremony and amputate an arm . . . the next year a leg—you get the picture. All the while they keep indoctrinating them. Finally nothing's left but a brain, with no place to go but into one of these ships."
> "What happened to this one?"
> "Maybe it just wasn't ready. Maybe the indoctrination didn't stick. You're the only one for sure who can find out what's going on in there.
> "In other words, you want me to play Annie Sullivan to your bionic Helen Keller."
> "A nice way to put it, yes. *If* you think you're up to the assignment."

Of course, Lara's psychic probing gets her closer to the brain than she bargained for. As the mental bond becomes tighter, so does her passion for the bodiless pilot.

> Zyglos was furious. "Admit it, Lara—you're in love with that thing. You're holding back information. It *could* be

called treason." She could feel him smirking, inwardly. He wasn't angry at all; it was something else entirely.

"I'm not holding back anything. I'm a psychiatrist, not a decoding machine. There's a person in there—or what's left of one. I have to deal with that first."

"You know what I think? I think you're enjoying your little fantasy affair with that piece of cauliflower. A real man might be too much . . . brain tissue *isn't* erectile, after all . . ."

"You stinking bastard," Lara cried. "You slimy woman-hating creep! You think *you* know what a woman needs?" She focused all her telepathic power on Zyglos's deepest sexual anxieties. "Shall we start with a recitation of your sexual failures, beginning at the age of nineteen? A systems analyst named Doris—"

"Shut up!" screamed the misogynist.

"And why don't we share this with the others? Here, the intercom—!"

The relationship between Lara and the brainship was depicted as infinitely preferable to anything that could be achieved between standard men and women. Her agent Cherie was ecstatic. But then, she was always ecstatic.

"It's brilliant, Gillian . . . you understand the science fiction reader perfectly. Terrified of sex but desperate for romance . . . craving *military* structure in relationships . . . and yet, so vulnerable and afraid! Do you have any idea of how far you can go with this?"

"Well, of course I'm pleased—"

"You ought to be pleased! But Gillian: do you realize what a *bombshell* you have in your relationship to Julian? I want you to come out of the closet. Write it! I could auction the book—"

"Cherie! Somehow I don't think my marriage is any match for that last well-publicized deal of yours." The agent was still high on the success of her $2 million paperback sale of a horror novel called *The Fucken*, about sexually accelerated children in suburbia. The title, which should have presented huge marketing problems, was instead transformed into a major asset. The novel sported jet-black covers with no copy, just a diagonal spatter mark in alternating red and white . . . readers could make the subliminal choice between blood and semen. The magazine and newspaper ads were even better. "We can't print the name of this novel. We don't have to. IT WILL FIND YOU." Splat.

Now Cherie was hoping for a movie deal for *Helen Keller in Outer Space*. She felt it would thematically capture the imagination of an audience weaned on sexless space fantasies and now looking for something stronger. Bodiless passion between humans and cyborgs would seem to be the winning ticket. But she wanted the publicity that would come from Gillian's betraying her husband.

"Honey, can't you see it? Your book has made you the high priestess of those zombies he crusades against! *Helen Keller in Outer Space* is supposed to be their bible."

"I want my anonymity. I'm not interested in exploiting my relationship to Julian."

"What are you talking about? You've already exploited him. That book was your way of kicking him in the balls, if you haven't noticed. He's an asshole. He *always* was an asshole. Is it that house in Marin you're worried about? Sweetie, you can write your own ticket now. Literally."

"Enough, Cherie! We're not blowing my cover, and that's final."

"What is it between you two, anyway? I should have known when two people named 'Julian' and 'Gillian' decided to get married, it was going to be difficult to pry them apart."

"All right, Cherie. I'm hanging up. This has been enough long-distance for one day."

"Okay. But do me a favor and just think about it. Just *think* about it."

"I'll think about it. Now can I go?"

"Thanks. Good-bye Gillian."

"Good-bye, Cherie."

Gillian switched off the cordless receiver. The last of the morning's fog was burning away, and Mount Tamalpais was framed perfectly by the kitchen window. So, too, would she be framed to an outside observer. Framed, fixed, trapped. Difficult to pry them apart . . . well, Cherie was right about that. Perhaps they could never be apart until she understood completely just why they were together. And somehow, *Helen Keller in Outer Space*, for all its commercialism and smart-ass glibness, was a step in that direction.

She poured herself yet another cup of espresso and put an album on the stereo, an old Dory Previn thing that was one of her personal favorites, but which no one else could stand. So here she was, listening alone, living the kind of life in the kind of house she had written about so often. Everything perfectly coordinated but nothing fitting together.

Maybe it was time for some messy vitality.

In the distance was the sound of an ambulance siren. It sounded like one of the Resurrection House wagons. So Julian was going to have another plaything, another fresh catch. San Francisco's supply was endless. Just once, Gillian thought, just *once* give him a nut that can't be cracked. Just once let him meet his match. And let it be a woman.

•

Deep inside a brain in a body that no longer mattered, Diandra sensed the reassuring motion of the machine, the siren's wail, the shapes of attendants huddling over her. Were they human or the other kind? *So this is Boca Verde*, she thought. Here they would give her the kind of life she wanted, the kind of life she deserved, a life beyond life. *A chance.*

But then she saw the sign above the gate, upside down as they passed:

AUTHORIZED PERSONNEL ONLY
RESURRECTION HOUSE

And was delivered into agony.

DIANDRA

"Julian . . . I want you to look at this . . . an unusual case
. . . a *very* unusual case."

"Unusual? I thought that was pretty much our cruis-
ing speed."

"I don't think I've ever seen one quite like this. A
withdrawal so *complete*. For a minute I wasn't sure she
was even—"

"Don't worry, she's human, just like the rest of them.
The hair, the makeup—you're right, they're startling
. . . she's gotten very, very deeply into this thing. But
not so deeply that we won't pull her out of it."

"Kicking and screaming, no doubt."

"No doubt. I think I'd like to handle this case myself.
And make sure Jensen in PR gets some pictures. You
know the kind I like."

•

Diandra heard voices. Or, rather, she *sensed* them
without making sense *of* them. The space around her
mind was like a diving bell. There wasn't much that
could get through.

35

There wasn't much she would let through.

She stared at the grid of the ceiling through half-opened eyes. The mechanical pattern reassured her. Cool artificial light came from everywhere and no-where. But appearances could be deceptive, she knew . . . she had to remain on guard. Could this really be Resurrection House? Her reaction to the sign had been instantaneous. She had, after all, been warned about deprogrammers—they had all been warned about those who could never accept the new reality and who would stop at nothing to destroy it. Like doomed, lumbering dinosaurs who could not make the next evolutionary step, they sought only to trample and destroy.

This room was just a holding pen, before they would start their damage.

Best, then, to remain very, very still.

•

On a summer afternoon twenty years before, there had been another room and another stillness. The room was the only room that Diandra could call her own from the time she was born until she left for college at the age of eighteen. It was a simple room, and orderly, not at all like her girlfriends' with their ruffles and stuffed toys and riotous 1950s "color con-spiracies" (*scheme* being too mild a word for the sen-sory inundation of electric pink and leopard skin in vogue among her peers). Diandra's room was convent-like in its austerity, and when she finally moved out after eighteen years, it was difficult to believe anybody had ever lived there at all.

In a way, nobody had, although for a while a young girl named Diandra seemed to inhabit the space. The house was in a medium-sized town in central Ohio, not far from Columbus, and the neighborhood was a post-war housing development without many trees. It was a long walk to any open space, the nearest being the grounds surrounding the public library, where Diandra spent a great deal of her time.

Diandra's family consisted of her mother, her father, and her mother's brother Steve, who moved in when Diandra was thirteen. Uncle Steve had had a twin brother who died when very young. Although Diandra didn't know anything of the circumstances, she sensed that her mother had felt some kind of guilt or responsibility for the surviving brother. It was a devotion that frequently sparked fights between her mother and father. Apparently, her father's salary was not keeping up with the booming postwar economy, and Uncle Steve's sporadic earnings (he called himself an "entrepreneur," whatever that meant) were needed to hold things together.

"In the next life, I'm going to do it differently," she heard her father say once, bitterly. "I'll stay in the army, out of the quicksand." Diandra assumed that she was part of the quicksand and never asked for anything she didn't need. Once she endured a toothache for three weeks before begging her mother to take her to a dentist. Her father was likely to fly into a rage at the suggestion of doctor's visits. Doctors were out to trick you and bleed you and make you come back for more. You were better off without them. "Please don't tell Daddy," she implored her mother. She was afraid he would try to remove the tooth himself, at home, for cheap.

Diandra disliked her name intensely. *Die*-andra, her parents pronounced it, often shortening it to a chilling directive: *Die*. "Di . . ." they would say to her. And no matter what the context or inflection, Diandra *would* die a little, believing all the more that her parents would have been happier if she had never been born.

Uncle Steve displayed more interest in her than either of her parents. He was a smiling, sweating man who wore flashy sportcoats, cuff links, and cologne. And yet, there was something oddly childlike about him. He didn't have, or at least he didn't talk about, girlfriends. Everything outside the house was business or the pursuit of business. But sometimes when Diandra listened to him talk about his deals and plans, it was like hearing a little boy playing at being grown-up. You never knew whether to believe him. But if it was all just a game, then it didn't matter.

Her mother, Lila, was given to emotional outbursts that frightened Diandra. Sometimes Diandra would come home from school and find her mother in the basement laundry room, sobbing amid a pile of unwashed clothes. "Spying on me, are you? Well, are you satisfied? Do you see now what it means to be a woman?"

Lila would make threatening references to the "changes" that were going to take place, soon, in Diandra's body. Changes that were apparently so terrible that she could not bring herself to describe them to her daughter in any fashion whatsoever. "Take it from me. It's going to be more trouble than it's worth. Enjoy your life while you can, kid; enjoy it while you're clean."

Diandra began to enjoy her life less. Between her mother's inability to cope, her father's drinking, and the threat of an impending biological catastrophe, she found a measure of safety in her books and in her sketchpads, which she filled with fantasy impressions of worlds apart from her own. She excelled in school, was a straight "A" student. It was one area of her life in which she was in control. So much in control, in fact, that the nuns who taught her had ceased to have words of praise and encouragement. She did everything that was expected of her, perfectly. And so became invisible.

At home the fights between her parents became more frequent and violent, often ending with the slamming of a door and the squealing of tires in the driveway. Diandra felt relief and fear simultaneously—relief that the fight was over and terror that her father was abandoning her to her mother. She hoped that her mother would be exhausted after these exchanges, but usually, just the opposite was true. The fights excited her more than ever, and if Uncle Steve wasn't around to stop her, she would come for Diandra.

"Die," her mother said. "I know you're awake. Come downstairs with me. It's time I showed you something."

"Mama, it's late—"

"I said it's time." And Diandra thought she heard a dry little laugh under her mother's words, like the crumpling of paper or the crackling of flames.

Diandra put on her robe and followed her mother down to the basement. Was Lila going to pull her down into a pile of dirty clothes? But Lila marched her past the laundry room and into the far shadows of the basement. It was dank and cold.

"Do you see it?"

"Mama, there's nothing. It's dark. Please let's go to bed."

"Look—over there." Diandra looked. And saw the old birdcage that had been abandoned to the corner since her parakeet died a year before. The little door hung open.

Lila smiled. "It's not empty. I've been growing something here for a long time."

Diandra felt the skin at the back of her neck tighten. Was her mother crazy?

"Here," said Lila, producing something from her robe pocket. It was wrapped in sandwich paper. Lila opened it, and Diandra could see pieces of beef suet and strips of fatty meat.

"The doctor told him to be careful, because of his blood pressure. So I have to feed it down here instead."

"Mama, please stop talking like this."

"Why? You might as well know. You can't see a heart attack until it happens, but it's growing all the same, growing and getting stronger in the dark. It's my only hope—"

Diandra fled the basement. Her mother was laughing and did not follow. Diandra blocked the door to her room with a chair and held a pillow over her ears to smother the craziness in the house, the craziness in her head.

One night, near the end of their time together as a family, Lila went into a rage at dinner. Diandra hadn't breathed a word to provoke her.

"You don't think I know what's on your mind? The kind of *questions* you're just dying to ask, here, every night at the table? Things that aren't any of your business!" She snatched away Diandra's plate and smashed it on the linoleum. "Look at me, Missy!" She grabbed Diandra under the chin, turned her head.

"Mama, no—" The flesh on her mother's arms was loose and pale. But her stare was firm and penetrating.

"You want to know so bad, don't you? About men? And women? Okay . . . I'll tell you. *We made you*. With our bodies! His thing and my thing! Are you satisfied?"

Lila released her and started to laugh. Diandra's father got up and left the room without a word. I'm not going to be part of this, thought Diandra. *His thing. Her thing.*

A few days later Diandra came home from school, dreading, as usual, the possibility of another upsetting scene with her mother. She imagined what it must be like to live alone, completely alone, with no parents or nuns or anyone at all to make her feel bad. She would make the rules. And she would never have to let anyone in if she didn't feel like it. Self-contained. Alone in a box.

Diandra's family's house was the box, squat, aluminum-sided, its door and windows forming a huge, astonished face in her imagination, a hectic clown or demon. The door was painted red. *Go ahead*, thought Diandra. *Eat me. See if I care.*

Diandra avoided the mouth, despite her inner bravado, and went to the side door instead. She hesitated, held her breath, then opened the door and went into the kitchen.

Uncle Steve was sitting at the rickety kitchen table, hunched over a cup of coffee.

"Where's . . . Mama?" stammered Diandra.

Uncle Steve smiled, even though a smile was clearly inappropriate. Something was wrong. Very wrong. Diandra dropped her book bag on the little utility table next to the broom closet. She sat down without removing the monogrammed jacket that said "St. Monica's."

"I have a little news, Dee . . . that's the way you like to say it, isn't it? You see, I noticed. Uncle Steve notices these things."

"What's wrong, Uncle Steve?" Had her mother finally succeeded with her birdcage . . . with the "thing" in the cellar?

"Your Mama's gone away for a little while," said Uncle Steve, sipping his coffee. Diandra stared at the flashy pinky ring as he set down the cup. She didn't want to hear any of this. But at the same time, she felt a swelling relief.

"Where did she go?" asked Diandra.

"She's gone to a kind of hospital . . . not the kind where they're going to operate on her or anything like that. Just a place where she can rest a bit. Until she feels like she's strong enough to come back."

"What's wrong with her?"

"Well, part of it's what's called 'the change of life,' and that means Lila's not going to be completely a woman anymore. Do you understand what that means?"

"No . . . I mean, I don't think so—"

Uncle Steve looked at her curiously. "How much do they tell you at school?"

Diandra flushed hotly.

"I guess those nuns don't tell you anything. I'm not

surprised. I don't know why Lila held on to that damn religion, why she forced it on you. I grew up with the nuns, too, and I hated every minute of it. I guess for girls it's different, the nuns being women too. At least, they're *sorta* like women. For me, I'd like to know exactly what they're hiding under all that sailcloth and starch."

"I don't know what you're talking about," said Diandra, not looking at her uncle.

"Then maybe we should start at the beginning," he said, reaching out his hand. "Your daddy won't be back 'til late. Don't worry. We have plenty of time."

•

Afternoons with Uncle Steve became a regular part of Diandra's life from then on. There was nothing she could do. She couldn't even bring it up in confession . . . for this was a special sin, she was convinced, one that would never be forgiven. Uncle Steve always whispered to her afterward what a tease she was, what a bad, bad girl for having started it all . . . even though Diandra didn't really *do* anything. She simply put up no resistance, let her mind go blank. She experienced those afternoons like a program on television. A young girl in a Catholic school uniform going through predictable series of motions. He always wanted her to keep on some of the uniform. It was important to him. Exciting. For Diandra's part there was no arousal, just detachment. She would imagine what it was like to be one of the nuns, women without bodies floating through the convent school on cushions of air. Cushions of faith. Women who didn't have to worry about men and their urges. Women who didn't have to exist in *this* world at all, only the next.

Uncle Steve brought her many presents during that time, most of which she ignored. There was one, however, that riveted her attention. It was a music box topped with a small figure of a ballerina; it swirled and pirouetted to a toy orchestration of the *Sleeping*

Beauty waltz. Its movements were unfailingly perfect, its demeanor imperturbable. *Some men like music*, Uncle Steve would cue her, and she would rise to wind the key and set the machine spinning on her dresser. The movements would hypnotize her as Uncle Steve pursued his satisfaction. That completed, she would often arise again to set the toy in motion once more, to occupy her senses while Uncle Steve dressed and prepared to leave.

"You really like that music box, don't you, Dee?"

"Yes."

"That ballerina . . . sometimes I think you like her more than me. Sometimes I think I have competition."

Diandra looked at her uncle blankly.

"Tell me . . . does she have a name?"

"Yes," said Diandra. "She's Dionne."

●

"College? What do you need to go away to college for? You can go to college here."

"It's not college. It's art school."

"It would be a lot cheaper for you to stay at home, I should think."

"I've won a scholarship. It will pay for everything. It would be more expensive to stay at home."

"You're doing this to get back at me, aren't you? To get away from me—"

"Please, Uncle Steve, don't start—"

"I think I've been pretty good to you. I don't think I deserve to be walked out on like this."

Diandra sat stiffly on her ladderback chair. She sat watching the figurine Dionne. Watching it spin, gracefully, effortlessly, in touch with a perfect mechanical universe contained beneath her feet. It was the only perfect thing in her life.

"Are you hearing anything I'm saying, Dee? Maybe your Mama and Daddy would be interested in hearing some things I have to say . . ."

Diandra spoke to him, her eyes not moving from the

music box. "My mother is in a state mental hospital, and my father is a drunk. I'm leaving them and I'm leaving you. You can tell them whatever you want. It doesn't matter anymore." The ballerina seemed to spin faster, a perfect gyroscope, in perfect control. Diandra, too, was in control.

"I've given up a lot for you, you know. Other men my age have lady friends—*real* lady friends, and wives and families. Damn you! Will you listen to me?"

And suddenly Uncle Steve moved in front of her, a raging blur, and before Diandra could say a word he snatched up the music box and hurled it against the bedroom wall. The little figure shattered on impact, the weight of the drive mechanism snapping Dionne's spine, her arms, her legs. Diandra felt her mouth opening in a silent scream. Pieces of Dionne were flying everywhere, little body parts terminating in screws and springs. The ruined toy fell to the bed, the spring in its final spasm. One of Dionne's legs was still attached to the drive shaft. It whipped around like a crazy snake.

No—

Can't lose Dionne—

And Diandra's mind opened up to rescue the soul of the toy, the only locus of peace she had known since Uncle Steve had taken over her life.

I won't let you go—ever—

Uncle Steve was sobbing at the end of the bed. "How can you do this to me? Isn't there anything I can do . . ."

Diandra stopped at the door and thought.

"There is one thing . . ."

"Yes . . ."

"After I'm gone . . ."

"Yes—"

"You could cut it off. And mail it to me."

•

Diandra detested New York. At first the idea had seemed glamorous. *Going to school in New York.*

Studying art in New York. But the reality of life in the East Village was far from the sparkling, cosmopolitan center of her imagination. Rather, it was a stinking, crawling place, full of things that skittered in the cupboards, things that fouled the sidewalks, things that crouched in doors and subways and seemed to be human but couldn't be, couldn't possibly. Diandra resolved to keep the city at a distance from touching her, and she spent most of her time at Cooper Union working on her classroom assignments, and other assignments, too—ones she gave herself to pass the time, to avoid going home to the dreary walk-up room on East 6th Street, with the roaches and the noise.

Her instructors would remember her as earnest but aloof; "a little too much in control" is how more than one of them put it. Diandra couldn't understand. She felt nowhere near being "in control." "Control" was something a long way off, if she could ever attain it. And yet everyone kept telling her that "control" was her problem. Her paintings and constructions, while precise, hard-edged, icy, strong and distinctive, were decidedly out of step with those of her classmates. It was a constant source of frustration that her uniqueness would be frowned upon by supposedly creative individuals. So she pulled into herself even more deeply.

When she finally graduated, it dawned on her with some dismay that the largest job market was, unfortunately, New York. Like it or not, she would be staying here awhile. She renewed her lease, paid for an expensive exterminator out of her precious food money, and painted the entire studio with white polyurethane—floors, walls, and ceiling, an impenetrable shield. Chitin all her own.

After a few free-lance jobs in midtown advertising agencies and design firms, she received a call from a magazine where she had left her portfolio. The magazine was *Fashion Plate*, one of the major glossies. She went to the editorial offices, high in a boxy building on Madison Avenue in the fifties, to meet Ardis Gallagher, the art director.

Ardis was a bright, handsome woman in her mid-forties, with large luminous eyes and a no-nonsense manner. She was impeccably dressed and groomed. "You understand that this is an entry-level position. There'll be a little bit of everything. Go-fer stuff, helping with layouts and shoots, some photo styling. It's varied and it's interesting. It's also a lot of work. Do you think you can handle it?"

"Yes. At least I think so."

"Good. Welcome aboard."

Diandra liked working at *Fashion Plate*. The offices were immaculate. The look of the magazine itself excited her—the "Swiss" style of art direction; austere, logical arrangements created on a rigid underlying structure known as a *grid*. Diandra liked the grid. It made her feel safe. It was something she could depend on. The magazine was a kind of machine, a precision clockwork. Ardis had won many design awards for her work at *Fashion Plate*, and they were displayed prominently in her office. Diandra sensed that Ardis, too, was dedicated to a certain amount of control in her life, and admired the extent to which she had been able to achieve it.

Three weeks after she had started work Ardis came over to her cubicle. "I'd like to have lunch with you, Diandra. Will one o'clock be all right?"

The unexpected abruptness of the invitation startled her. Was she going to be fired? What had she done? She strained to recall any incident, any cause for a reprimand. But there was nothing. A cold, sick dread settled over her. She met Ardis at one o'clock outside her office.

"No, you didn't do anything. I always take my new girls out to lunch. Get to know them better. God knows, you can lose track of the *people* in this madhouse."

Diandra managed a little laugh. Ardis took her to a lunch spot fashionable with the advertising and design crowd. The decor was high-tech, the cuisine *nouvelle*, the service flawless.

"You have talent," said Ardis near the end of the lunch. "Your portfolio was one of the most striking I've seen in a long time. So interesting . . . almost all images of women . . . *superwomen*, in a way. Those android nuns—brilliant! And the ballerina with the windup key in her back. All women . . . and in a way, women who are *more* than women."

Ardis downed the last of her coffee. "I can help you, Diandra. I really can. More than that, I *want* to."

"I'm flattered."

"Don't be. I have my own reasons."

She leaned forward, lowering her voice.

"You know, of course, there's a very strong sexual element in hiring."

Diandra froze. She was no longer in a chic Manhattan restaurant. She was not being propositioned by a lesbian art director. She was back in Ohio, *on* her back, the weight of her Uncle Steve crushing out her breath, the thick pulsing fact of him splitting her open . . .

There had been no place for her to run. And now, there was no place for her to run.

"I'm . . . I'm afraid I'm not . . . interested—"

Ardis waved for the check. "Not interested? I know you're not interested in *men*. I've seen you with some of the hunks in the office, and you're inert."

"I'm not interested in women *or* men. I'm just not interested, period."

"I see," said Ardis, smiling. "In time, then. There's no hurry. Would you like some more coffee?"

•

The panic that descended on Diandra was unlike

anything she had felt since Ohio, since her Uncle Steve
and the bare bedroom in that clapboard house of mad-
ness. Ardis kept her distance at work; there was nothing coercive about her manner, nothing that could be
construed as harassment. Just a cool professional mask.
But behind the mask, Ardis had made her claim. Diandra's breath grew constricted whenever Ardis came
near. She didn't understand lesbianism. She didn't understand sex of any kind and didn't want to. Suction.
Friction. The body and its secretions. But the art director had given her some kind of ultimatum, the consequences of which she must escape at any cost.

It was nearing Christmas, and so there were an endless series of office parties, receptions, and open
houses. Diandra preferred to stay home with her
sketchpads. Christmas had some reassuring connota-
tions . . . the possibility, for instance, of virgin birth.
Existence without sex. She labored for several nights
over some technical drawings that even she found
strange. Blueprints for a mechanical Madonna. A baby-
making machine. But the results were so disturbing,
stirring religious guilt she thought she had escaped
long ago, that she tore the drawings up, never showing
them to anyone.

One Friday, Diandra visited a Park Avenue gynecolo-
gist with a minor complaint. A friend at *Fashion Plate*
had recommended him.

The afternoon was cold and rainy. A freezing wind
rattled the doctor's examining room window. The doctor had a pinched expression and his hands were cold.
After he finished examining her, she disengaged herself
from the stirrups and dressed.

"You know," said the doctor, washing his hands,
"you could save yourself a lot of trouble later by having
it all taken out now."

"What . . . do you mean . . . ?"

"A prophylactic hysterectomy. We do them all the

time now. No more periods, no more complications.
There's only trouble down the road, you know." The
doctor sat behind his desk, forearms on the blotter. He
held a pencil in his hands, and Diandra imagined that
he was about to break it, like a breadstick.

The wind howled.

"Yes," said Diandra, impulsively. "Yes, I think you're
absolutely right. I want it all taken out."

The doctor seemed to relax a bit. He released the
pencil, and something like a smile came over his face.

"Wh-when can I . . . I mean, how *soon* can we—?"

"Good girl," said the doctor. And it *was* a smile.

•

A few weeks later, at an office function she could not
avoid, she caught the eye of a handsome, seamlessly
stylish man from the West Coast. He introduced himself—his name was Philip—and Diandra felt instantly at
ease. This man would demand nothing of her, at least
not *that* way. She accepted another glass of wine. Talking became easier.

" . . . and the store I'm from, Croesus in San Francisco, is doing some very interesting work in visual
marketing. Trailblazing, I hope. Similar in style to some
of these features you've worked on for *Fashion Plate*."

"San Francisco. It must be nice."

"It is nice. Very nice. You should try it sometime."

"I'd like to leave New York. I've been here quite
awhile, now. I went to school here."

Philip seemed to sense something in her voice. He
looked at her in a different way over his glass. Talked in
a more conspiratorial tone.

"You're not one of Ardis's . . . by any chance?"

"You . . . might put it that way."

"Oh, I see. Then there's absolutely no question about
it. You *must* leave New York."

They both laughed, a little tipsy from the Char-
donnay.

"I've known Ardis for a long, long time, my dear, and I can assure you that the situation you are in, or in which you may soon find yourself, will do nothing to enhance your fortunes. Look, I'll give you my card. And if you think you're serious about moving to San Francisco, give me a call. And we'll talk."

Diandra gave her notice, had the hysterectomy between Christmas and New Year's, and moved to San Francisco the second week in January. *Such a clean city*, she thought, in wonderment, upon her arrival. From the twin peaks overlooking the city, it appeared gleaming white, sunbaked. How unlike the East, with its contagion and filth. She walked around the city in a daze for weeks, disbelieving. The people were clean, too; unusually well-groomed and fashion-conscious. How unlike New York and its unwashed millions, the heavy layer of grime that clung to every surface, fingers of dirt waiting to streak you at every turn.

San Francisco was a glittering toy, an innocent playpen. She had not been so happy since her early childhood. One day was like another: fog in the morning that burned off by noon, dazzling sunlight the rest of the time. Only in winter did it rain, but the rain was clean, too. There were no extremes in temperature. You were not so aware of your body and its discomforts. This, perhaps, was the most welcome aspect of life in San Francisco. She didn't have to think about her body at all, and the city was full of the kind of men who would make no physical claims. They gravitated instinctively to her, and she to them. The diversity of gay life surprised her—such a complete cross section of humanity that had somehow evolved beyond breeding. To be sure, she was aware, dimly, that they *did* things, things she didn't consider specifically. But surely these were momentary lapses of faith. All in all, the tone was right. And whatever they did with each other, they weren't going to do anything to *her*. No one would touch her. It seemed civilized, very advanced, in keep-

ing with the sparkling technological age they in-
habited.

In those first months in San Francisco, much of the
tension that had plagued her since Ohio lifted a bit. She
stopped panicking every time a man brushed her on
the crowded sales floor of I. Magnin or Croesus. She
stopped seeing the ghost of her Uncle Steve lurking in
bars. He was dead in fact, dead for years, shut down by
a heart attack the summer of Mount St. Helens. Diandra
couldn't help but wonder if the coronary was the
creepy cardiac delusion her mother had kept in the
cellar, and had somehow escaped, killing the wrong
man. Diandra's father had written about it in a Christmas card, along with the annual news that her mother
was no better, work was slow, and she was missed. She
didn't believe her father. She didn't know who her
father was—why should she? Year after year the letters
became shorter and terser. But they didn't stop. Knowing that there was no way to halt them altogether,
when she left New York she simply reported no for-
warding address.

Both family and uterus were consigned to the dead
letter office of the New York Postal Authority.

The job in the display department at Croesus came
surprisingly fast. Philip was impressed by the styling
and conceptual work evident in her portfolio from
Fashion Plate; many of her assignments were elaborate
and three-dimensional; the transition to visual retail
merchandising was a natural one.

Her work caused a stir . . . a needed stir, since the
department store's reputation had been lagging for
years behind the more illustrious San Francisco empo-
ria. The complete architectural renovation of the
building's handsome California/Deco facade and interiors provided public relations impetus.

Philip described the strategy. "Art Deco—the machine aesthetic, right? What we want to do now is
bring it up to date. The machine then and now—but

mostly *now*. High tech—the *highest* tech. Robots, computers, E.T., anything goes. But it has to have style, and it has to look like no other department store in the world. Here, look at these."

He unrolled some sketches of the direction he wanted the store to take. The renderings looked more like Disneyland or EPCOT Center than any retail center.

'You could practically charge admission," said Diandra.

"And eventually we will. In the future, shopping will become a major form of entertainment. Look at print media now. It's nothing but ads, excuses for ads, backup for ads. Go to any newsstand. What do you see? What to buy. Where to spend, how to think. There's no real journalism anymore, but people pay for it anyway. Croesus will become a tourist attraction as well as a merchandising outlet."

"But won't people resist having to *pay* for the privilege to *buy*—?"

"There'll be some objections, but it can only help, in terms of publicity. It will make us seem all the more exclusive. Nothing will be able to keep them away. Nothing."

There was something delightfully perverse about Philip's enthusiasm. Was he a crackpot or really onto something? Sometimes Diandra couldn't be sure. Like Diandra, Philip was a transplanted New Yorker and projected the same overpowering aura of hyperactive ambition she had seen time and again among men and women who had come west. They moved faster than their Californian counterparts, always asking why things couldn't be accomplished quicker. Is so-and-so *still* out to lunch? Didn't people care about their careers, didn't people want to *accomplish* anything? he complained. They had a different sense of humor; he often had to explain jokes. East Coast intensity could put people off socially but was a terrific asset in business.

Diandra enjoyed the intensity, the sense of pushing back limits. One of her first windows received a controversial notice in Herb Caen's column in the *San Francisco Chronicle*; the writer questioned whether or not Diandra's nightmare imagery of women mutating into refrigerators and food processors was really appropriate for Union Square or might better be relegated to the midnight movie circuit.

She liked the attention. She also liked the imagery itself. Philip had the marketing sense, but Diandra had the visual concepts. Philip could plan, but Diandra had the ability to shock. To attract the attention of the media, to stop people cold on the street. And for every customer who walked off the sales floor in disgust or horror, another ten would come flooding through the revolving silver gates.

Diandra was happy.

Diandra was *in control*.

One night at a party Philip had invited her to, an elegant-decadent soirée near the crest of Divisadero Street overlooking the Marina, Diandra was approached by the hostess, a woman draped in shroud-like bolts of iridescent fabric. Her lustrous hair was crowned with a tiara patterned after the 1930s grill-work of the Chanin Building in New York.

I like her style, Diandra thought.

And almost simultaneously realized that the woman had no arms.

"You're Diandra, aren't you? I'm so glad I convinced Philip to bring you. I'm Venus. Venus Tramhell."

The woman's escort, a Japanese businessman well known in San Francisco boardrooms, excused himself. In lieu of extending a hand, Venus stood close—too close—and fixed Diandra with a nearly unblinking stare of her grey-green eyes. This subtle intrusion on personal space was apparently her means of territorial contact. Venus? No, *Veronica* Tramhell, and Diandra remembered: the avant-garde sculptress, the headlines, the horrible accident with the industrial lasers she was using in her work. But she had risen from her own ashes, celebrating her disfigurement, renaming herself after the world's most famous statue in a *coup de theatre* of public relations. Now a patron and producer, she was a powerful figure in the California and New York art worlds. Diandra thought of the press photos of her many appearances at charity benefits and auctions, resplendent and startling in her Halston caftans, disabled but defiant.

"The work you're doing with Philip is truly extraordinary, Diandra. It's a whole new art form."

"Well, we try to be original."

"Just try? No, my dear . . . it's more than original. You've managed to turn the tables on merchandising. Instead of serving the product, the product serves *you*. Your sensibility intrigues me, Diandra. Do you have any formal training in cybernetics? The relationship between men and machines?"

"No, I, uh, just studied art. And read a lot of science fiction."

"Then your insights are basically instinctive. And all the more important."

"Really, I think of my work as purely commercial."

"Of course you do. And it's fine for you to think that. Just keep doing it. The world needs your images."

"Why, thank you."

Venus moved closer, and Diandra could sense the compensatory effort with which she kept her balance. "Diandra, would you come with me to my office? Yes, right now—it's just down the hall. I have something I'd like to show you. Something you really should see."

•

Diandra followed Venus to her inner sanctum, a bay-windowed room with a spectacular view over the Palace of the Legion of Honor. She turned on the overhead track lighting by tapping a foot switch; Diandra noticed that there were dozens of such switches all throughout the house to accommodate its mistress's special requirements.

Fully lit, the room was revealed as a plushly carpeted, grey and silver den dominated by a massive onyx desk, a wall of framed memorabilia. The mood was moderne, a Norman Bel Geddes fantasy of 1934. A self-contained projection television stood opposite the bay window, a machine out of its time. Venus turned to face her, and the movement of her caftan caused one of the slitted sides to open briefly, revealing one of her puckered stumps in a way that was both provocative and vaguely indecent. Diandra thought of the nuns who had shaped her childhood, *their* swirling raiment. And bodies that may not have existed at all.

"I'd like to play you something, Diandra. I'd like to know what you think." She tapped a series of switches in a little dance like that of a circus horse counting. The lights dimmed, and the video screen shimmered with projected light. Diandra heard the whir of a video-tape machine.

What followed began in the familiar format of a rock-music video. A heavy, rhythmic beat . . . a pulsation. Imagery: crowded city streets in ponderous slow motion. Disaster scenes. The Bomb. Twentieth-century angst in all its manifestations. The singing, when it began, was a synthesized voice, neither male nor female, the voice of a machine. *New bodies for old/The truth will finally be told/The time has come/There'll be salvation for some/New bodies for old. . . .*

As the song built in intensity, so too the images grew stronger and more strangely juxtaposed. Scenes of death and violence alternated with clips from old science fiction movies . . . the creation of the robotress from Fritz Lang's *Metropolis* . . . the snap, crackle, and pop of antiquated special effects . . . Flash Gordon fantasies of invincible machines . . .

"Interesting, isn't it? Rather like one of your windows, I should think . . ."

"I see what you mean," said Diandra. There was something compelling about the tape. Something elusive and powerful. "It's using subliminals, isn't it?"

"You think so?" asked Venus.

Diandra watched. The lyric repeated over and over. It was like a chant or mantra. And as she watched and listened, she became aware of a deeper message, one that became clearer as the video achieved a soothing stroboscopic intensity.

"Just relax," said Venus. "Let yourself go."

Let myself go. Yes. Exactly.

Diandra let herself go.

"Hello," said a voice that seemed very familiar, although she had never heard it before. "Welcome to the Cybernetic Temple."

"Welcome," echoed Venus, very near yet very far away.

"You have been chosen to hear this message because it has been determined that you are possessed of special qualities . . . qualities that set you apart from other people and make you uniquely suited to understand its meaning. *You* are unique. You deserve to hear what you are about to hear, and the more you relax the more you will be able to hear and understand. And so take a deep breath now and let it out, and feel yourself growing more receptive and more relaxed, more deeply relaxed than you have ever imagined was possible . . .

"Ever since the beginning of man's history on Earth, the individual has had to face the inevitability of his own oblivion. Death has claimed all, the evolutionary life span of the physical body falling far short of the mind's vast potential. Until modern times, man could

only cling to the vague promises of religious salvation
. . . all lies, of course, of staggering proportions, but lies
with at least a grain of truth. For while religion could
hold out hope, it could not offer the *technology* of
personal salvation.

"The Cybernetic Temple offers personal salvation.

"The Cybernetic Temple Combines religion with
science.

"The Cybernetic Temple offers modern man a
chance to escape the limitations of the physical body.
The technology exists. Only government regulations
and an obtuse repressive medical establishment pre-
vent you from reaping the benefits. In future messages
we will tell you the TRUTH of the conspiracy to rob you
of your birthright . . . the right not to die.

"The Temple is everywhere. You will have no trouble
finding Worship. You will commune in the privacy of
your own home through the medium of videocassette.
Since there are many who are hostile to our goals it is
important to maintain a certain degree of public
discretion.

"This concludes your introduction to the Cybernetic
Temple. If you can still hear this message, you are
sufficiently receptive to continue your pilgrimage. Our
next message will reach you soon."

Diandra stood rock-still as the videocassette finished
and the projection screen filled with coruscating snow.
It was like the dead zone after the final test pattern, a
state of media limbo between darkness and dawn. She
was aware of the presence of Venus Tramhell behind
her, the rustle of fabric falling away. And then she
heard—or thought she heard—another sound: the sliding of a closet door, a clanking of apparatus, the tapping of a floor switch, buckles, and harnesses snapping
into place. A nightmare being outfitted for a ride. Diandra stared blankly. Her spine stiffened as the nipples of
Venus brushed her back. And from a great distance in

her mind she felt or dreamed she felt cool mechanical arms encircling her, stroking her, kneading her in a way that no human hands ever could, or ever would.

HOUSEWIVES, IN DEEP HYPNOSIS

The Silicon Valley housewife leans forward in the chair that cups her. "You're going to tell me it's all my fault, aren't you?" She is agitated, more excited than is her custom. Her coral-painted nails dig into her palms. Her breath is quick and shallow. Cocaine, perhaps? Not likely in this case, though you never can tell. You see them all the time now, these snow-packed Californians. Hungry. Like time-warped refugees from the Donner Party on a detour through Aspen.

But no. This agitation is different. It has been growing steadily in the six months you have been treating her, although nominally it is her fourteen-year-old son who is "the patient" and currently committed to your care. But she is equally in need. The Silicon Valley Housewife—you *think* of her as *The Silicon Valley Housewife*, just as you think of other patients and members of their families as *The Cupertino Computer Salesman* or *The Sausalito Securities Analyst* or *The Mill Valley Food Stylist*. In the back of your mind, you know that she has a name; it is *Mrs. Kreyche*, she is

Sheila Kreyche, and her son's name is Jason. The circumstances have estranged the father. Six months ago
Jason and his mother collided in a way that delivered
them unto you. Inevitably. Inexorably. You believe in
fate. In particular, you believe in your own destiny,
more than anything in the world.

"You think it's me to blame—that I'm the one who
did it." Tears gather in her green eyes. Characteristi-
cally, you have no tissues available to her or any of your
clients. The body and its secretions cannot be wiped
away. Not here. Not in your clinic. The Silicon Valley
Housewife holds her tense pose and chair's edge until
it is clear you will not respond. Then she succumbs to
gravity and the angle of chair. Egg-shaped, it cradles
her.

"I want you to hypnotize me again," she says.

"You know how to hypnotize yourself. If there's anything you want to recall—"

She bites her lip and looks away. She has a strong
profile, more handsome than pretty. Her skin glows in
the rubious light that reflects from your walls. They are
painted a uterine red, hung with primitive masks and
fetishes. A neo-brutalist slab of a desk separates you
from the woman in the egg chair.

"I can recall everything. I just want to understand
it."

"You seem to want my judgment. My punishment."

You choose the word carefully. It is the first time you
have used it, fully cognizant of the rippling associa-
tions. Power. Sex. Control and subservience. Perhaps it
is time to more fully explore these nuances with The
Silicon Valley Housewife. Sheila, wife of Kreyche. And
mistress of none.

"I want you to help me."

"Help you or help Jason?"

"I'm beginning to wonder if it's possible to help him.
It's been so many months."

"Jason is a very disturbed boy."

"When I saw what he looked like today . . . his eye almost swollen shut. You've been beating him, haven't you? And the smell—"

"We need to break through by whatever means we can. And surely whatever we do at Resurrection House can't compare to what he's already done to himself."

She closes her eyes and begins to breathe deeply. Silently, she is counting backward, transporting herself in time to that afternoon last spring when her life fell apart. You have accompanied her there a dozen times or more, guiding her, protecting her, allowing her to explore the incident, its prelude and aftermath; desensitizing her, enabling her to enter an event in her own life like a detached observer, examining it from every possible perspective. It has become a kind of psychic Zapruder film, as much your obsession as hers, an irresistible dance. Your partner, however, is hypnotically comatose; the waltz will be cerebral. Her mind is dilated, expectant and waiting, the legs of her unconscious spread wide. Marketing research has shown that housewives, in deep hypnosis, associate the scents of certain dishwashing detergents with the smell of semen . . . you will keep such facts in mind as you begin your explorations.

"Where are you, Sheila?"

There is a long pause before she speaks, but the voice, when it comes, is clear and strong. "I'm in the driveway. I'm in the car and turning into the driveway of my house."

"I want you to remember things very slowly, Sheila. That way we can stop whenever we want. Imagine that all your memories are on a videocassette—" (You catch yourself, stopping just short of asking her to imagine herself to *be* a VCR. That would simply be too much. Or . . . would it? Later, perhaps.) "We can move the tape forward or backward, as slowly or quickly as

we want. We can make things stop. We can look at
another tape. We can do anything we want. We are in
complete control."

"Control . . . yes."

"Control is very important to you, isn't it, Sheila?"

"If you don't control things, things control you."

"What are you controlling now, Sheila?"

"The car. I am controlling the car. The car in the
driveway. The driveway of my house."

You needn't ask her about the house; she has described it often enough. A sun-drenched bungalow of
suburban stucco, theme-park Spanish, a verdant green
wafer for a yard.

"Where are you coming from?"

"Shopping. I've been to the shopping center. To buy
things."

"Things?"

"For my kitchen."

"Not for your family?"

"No. Just for my kitchen. And me."

Her nipples stiffen under the synthetic blouse. The
kitchen always excites her, though she represses heavily outside the trance state. "Tell me about the
kitchen," you ask her. "Just freeze the car there in the
driveway and change channels for a minute. And tell
me about your relationship. With the kitchen."

"It's my favorite room in the house. In any house."

"Go on."

"I designed it myself. There were contractors, of
course, but *I* made all the decisions."

"You mean you were in control?"

"Yes. Completely in control."

And completely controlled, you scrawl absently on
your pad. You rarely take notes. These families are all
the same. So boringly predictable. And they think
they're so special. She catalogs the contents of her
temple: the microwave ovens, the food processors, the

coffee machine and its three-setting grinder, the personalized talking refrigerator ("Your ice cubes will be ready at 4:59, Sheila. I hope you enjoy your aerobics class."), the microfiche recipe retrieval system containing more dishes than her family could be force-fed in a lifetime, the household computer that controls everything from the air conditioner to the light dimmers to the checking account, the cordless telephone that doubles as a domestic surveillance system, the dishwasher, the trash compactor, the garbage disposal orifice in the stainless steel sink.

Supplications to the Machine God.

Everything that is not stainless steel is white. She describes the effect of the high California sun as it floods the room through the skylight of her technological ice palace. Glinting, blinding, dancing. "A whiter white than . . . white," she murmurs, and you cannot tell if she is mimicking a soap powder commercial or imagining the epicenter of a nuclear blast. Either way, you imagine her transfigured in her kitchen, beatified as if by Industrial Light & Magic. *Ritual purification*, you scribble.

"The kitchen seems to be perfect, Sheila."

"Perfect, yes."

"But what about the rest of the house? And the people in it?"

"There's no one else. No one but me."

"Your husband?"

Silence.

"And Jason? What about Jason?"

"Jason—" She begins to gasp.

"It's all right, Sheila. What about Jason?"

"He . . . he . . ."

"Yes?"

"He isn't—"

"Isn't?"

"Human."

"Now, Sheila, of course he's human. He's your son."
She shakes her head violently. "No. Not anymore."

"How did things change? When did you first notice?"

"A year ago, I guess. The videos. I don't know where
he got them. In school, I suppose. He was always
watching videos, you know, *Star Trek* and MTV. So I
didn't know that these were different. I couldn't even
stay in the room when he played them. I got such
headaches."

Denial, you write. She was fascinated by them. Could
she be faking the trance?

"We know now what those tapes were, Sheila. He
was being brainwashed."

"But what could I do? If he didn't watch them at
home, he'd just watch them somewhere else. All his
friends watched videos, played computer games—"

"What about *your* computer, Sheila?"

Silence. Then: "He didn't learn it from me."

"Now I want you to get back in the car, and we're
going to take you through the scene again. You're pulling into the driveway. What happens next?"

"The garage door opens. It's automatic."

"That's right. The whole house is automatic. You feel
protected. You feel safe."

"The door closes behind me and locks. I open the
hatch to get the bag—"

"The things you bought for the kitchen—"

"Yes. Some disinfectant spray, some paper towels.
Not much, really. Not worth the trip. Except—"

"Except that Jason was at home, and you *had* to get
away? Get away and buy things for the kitchen rather
than stay there and be alone in the house with your
son?"

"He's still there. The door to the kitchen is open, and
I can hear the sound."

"The sound?"

"The garbage disposal. I'm holding the car keys in

one hand and the store bag in the other. And I think, why is he running the garbage disposal? He barely even eats—"

"Now I want you to move very, very slowly toward the kitchen door. Just remember that we're in complete control here and nothing can happen to you. We're just watching a movie, and we can turn it off whenever we like. But I want you to go past the door this time and tell me what you see."

"Slowly . . ."

"Yes."

"It's like moving underwater . . . I take three—no, four—steps from the car to the kitchen door. The noise is very loud. I don't even look at him at first. I go directly to the counter at the opposite side of the room. There is a stain on the floor, coffee, I think. I set down the bag and hang the keys on their hook, and as I turn, I start to say something to Jason, loudly, in order to be heard."

"And then?"

She stalls.

"What do you see, Sheila?" You have a pretty good idea of what she sees, although there's some essential detail she has always held in. This time you will force it out.

"Sheila. What's going on? What is Jason doing?"

"B-bending—"

"Yes, bending where?"

"Over the sink—"

"And what is he doing, bending over the sink?"

"N-no, I can't—"

"Yes you can, Sheila. Take it one frame at a time. One still picture after another. Single-frame advance."

"His head is in the sink."

"And?"

"At first I think he's sick. That he's vomiting in the sink and using the motor to cover the sound. But he's not sick. Not being sick."

"What do you see, Sheila?"

"He's . . . licking it."

"It?"

"Them. The flaps. The rubber flaps on the disposal. He has the motor on and he's . . . *licking* them . . . like . . . like . . ."

"Go on, Sheila. Like what?"

"You know like what!"

Her entire body shudders. You watch the gooseflesh rise as it might in the frigid air-conditioning of a Cupertino supermarket.

"What do you see now, Sheila?"

"His hips . . . he's grinding his hips. I can hear him, just barely over the sound of the motor. Grunting. Moaning."

"And then?"

"He sees me."

You see him, too. A thin boy with a preternatural pallor. Blonde hair, ice-blue eyes, the brows so fine and thin as to be almost nonexistent. You can imagine the look on his face, the startling amalgam of fear and rage. Mostly rage. His piercing gaze you know intimately from your encounters in his present enclosure. The unmistakable, riveting stare of a fanatic.

"And what does he see when he sees you?"

"I'm . . . screaming. Screaming his name. I'm frightened, but I must look very angry. But he just looks at me with his own fury and contempt. How can my own son hate me so? I run to grab him. To slap him, to shake him up. Something. But then he makes a fist and shoves it in my face, and I think, my God, he's going to kill me."

"But he doesn't kill you."

"No. He just keeps staring at me, unblinking. He pulls the fist back. And for some reason, just at that moment I notice that he's wearing this *Star Trek* T-shirt. 'The

Wrath of Khan.' And I think, is *this* it? Is this the Wrath of Khan? And Jason looks at me like I'm nothing, a worm."

" 'You ruin everything,' he says. And then—"

"Yes?"

"He takes his fist—"

"Yes?"

"And jams it down the disposal."

She speaks calmly now, genuinely detached. This part you have been over many times. Only the specifics of the prelude were new. Now you realize that as Jason reaches into the disposal he is reaching into *her*.

"He doesn't feel anything," Sheila says matter-of-factly. "He just keeps looking at me like nothing's happening at all. That look of hatred. My baby with all that hate. The blood is flying everywhere. It's a mist, really, a warm mist of blood. I can see his arm, vibrating like a jackhammer as the disposal eats his hand. I go to him. I pull him away from the sink, and then there really *is* blood, then, on the floor, on the walls. We're spinning in it . . . it's almost like dancing. He has the stump between my breasts, and he's moving it up and down, so I can feel the spurts in my face. He screams that I'm a fucker, a bag of guts, that I was 'born meat,' and by that time we're rolling on the floor. Somehow there's a window broken. I grab for a towel to stop the blood. There's blood in my hair. There's blood up my nostrils. I've never smelled blood before, not like this. Never like this.

"He's still screaming at me when the neighbors come. I guess I'm yelling, too. We must be making an awful lot of noise, because I don't even hear the sirens, and everybody knows that ambulances use sirens.

"But I do notice when they turn off the disposal. The silence as they're strapping us onto the stretchers. That I notice.

"At the hospital they tell me that there was so much

blood on me that they supposed I was the victim. 'Aren't I?' I ask, but no one answers. 'Your son is going to be all right,' they tell me, and I know this is another misperception."

(She is quite probably right. Only yesterday you visited Jason in his pen. Even the most extreme deprogramming techniques have had little effect thus far. He squatted in the corner like some kind of feral child, protecting his bandaged stump. "It's not going to grow back," you told him. "You're going to have to live with this. Live with what you've done." "That's fine," he snarled back. "I can wait." "Wait?" you ask. He brandished the arm, like a torch awaiting the flame. "Yes. For something better.")

Sheila returns from her trance, greatly refreshed. "I found something I wanted to show you. With Jason's things." She hands you a heavily creased piece of paper. A document that had been hidden somewhere, folded and stuffed. You open it. It is a kind of blueprint for a mechanical hand. The concept is almost completely absurd; Jason has envisioned a kind of combination home entertainment center and death-ray weapon. A flat, flexible television screen is embedded in the palm. There are various plugs and hookups; he obviously sees himself as a component in a larger, expandable system. The index finger is a laser gun. The middle finger, most revealingly, has a duct at the tip that is marked "LUBRICANT." You almost laugh aloud. Perhaps he's not so far gone after all, if his fantasies included this. The rest of the paper is covered with meaningless combinations of mathematical symbols, a typically schizophrenic touch.

"I thought you should see this."

"It's quite . . . revealing."

"It was folded up inside a book. That paperback novel, the one they all read. *Helen Keller in Outer Space*."

"Yes, I know. Trash. Dangerous trash."

"The writer should be shot."

"As I understand it, they don't know who the writer is. He uses a pseudonym. But in all fairness, the book didn't start all this; it just exploited a terrible situation and made it worse."

"Terrible, yes . . ." she says distractedly, and you realize that she's stalling for time. Avoiding your gaze.

"Is there something else you wanted to discuss today?"

She bites her lip. "It's embarrassing."

"Oh?"

"I . . . I guess some of it came out, in the hypnosis. It's just that, ever since the . . . accident, I've been having . . . difficulties. Sexual difficulties."

"Can you be more . . . specific?"

"With oral sex. I mean, letting myself be—"

"Because you think of Jason? And what it was like?"

"What it reminded me of. Yes."

"And you want me to help you with this problem?"

"Is there anything that can be done?"

"It's probably just another matter for desensitization. Using whatever means are necessary to keep your mind off that image. When you do the thing it reminds you of."

"I want you to use whatever means are necessary," she says. She slides into position on the desk. The neo-brutalist slab of a desk. Her heels catch the edge like a stirrup.

"My methods may be . . . unorthodox."

"I know."

"But you still want—?"

"You know what I want. Just don't treat me like a . . ."

"Bag of guts? A piece of meat?"

You startle her. "No. I don't want you to treat me like a machine."

You laugh. "Don't worry about that. Never that."

And you strike her across the mouth with the back of your hand. A flesh-and-blood hand. Jason's face presses out momentarily behind her own. Wild, mad, accusing. You hit her again.

GILLIAN

Gillian, of course, had a lover. His name was Josh Seidelman, and he lived in Berkeley. He lived in Berkeley because it was one of the few cities in the country that was almost completely wheelchair-accessible. He also lived in Berkeley because he had always lived in Berkeley. Josh was a paraplegic. He hadn't been when Gillian first began seeing him a few years earlier. There had been an accident. The relationship became strained. But it lasted.

"I read in the paper that your husband's being sued for a billion dollars by the parents of one of those kids he was trying to deprogram. It seems he convinced them that it was hopeless unless they'd actually agree to fuck in front of the little zombie. And Julian, of course. The fucking was supposed to create some kind of 'primal scene' to snap the kid out of it. But the kid still thinks he's R2D2, and Mom and Dad haven't been able to have sex ever since." Josh steered his motorized chair over to the kitchen table, bringing with him a fresh carafe of coffee.

"Julian is always being sued by someone," said Gillian. "He writes off the losses as publicity expenses."

"And you're still married to that shit."

"Josh, let's not start—"

"But we've already started. You don't love him. You're just spoiled by the money and the house."

"The houses."

"Right. Let's not forget about the beach place."

"Josh, I did love him once. He used to be someone else."

"He was always the same person. He just needed California to encourage him. Forget him. Forget Connecticut. It was a different life."

"It's the same life. I don't know any different kind of life—"

"*This* isn't different enough for you?" He wheeled around and whirred over to the trash bin to dump the grounds and filter. "Christ, you're practically a best-selling novelist, or at least an underground best-seller. You can make it on your own." *Or with me.*

"The book was some kind of accident. Maybe I'll never write anything again. Cherie wants me to write a book about Julian. An exposé. Sleaze."

"Great. I love sleaze. Do it and get it out of your system. Get *him* out of your system." Gillian sensed his tone growing ugly. Low, scudding clouds of anger. "Or is that what you were trying to do with me and that novel? Write a story about a woman in love with a man who's half-machine? I take back my advice. Obviously, writing doesn't exorcise anything for you."

"Josh, you're being unfair. The book was a fantasy. And maybe it *was* about you, and me, and Julian and his obsessions. I wasn't even serious about publishing it."

"Well, you published it. And Julian seems to be getting more mileage out of it than you."

"I never thought anyone would take it seriously. I mean, it was science fiction."

"When will you start understanding that we're *living* science fiction, Gillian? Just read the papers. Actually, I think you do understand a lot more than you're willing to admit."

"Admit what, exactly?"

"Anger. No—make that rage. And perversity. For starters."

"I'm not angry, Josh." But she could feel the anger welling. "And as for rage and perversity, you've pretty much cornered the market." She glanced around the room at the framed copies of his award-winning political cartoons and advertising parodies. "I'll never forget this one," she said, indicating an ersatz magazine spread advertising Sunny Von Bulow designer sheets ("Linens so luxurious you'll *never* get out of bed.")

"You weren't supposed to forget it. That was the point."

"Stop goading me, Josh."

"Why? Because I'm backing you into a corner? Because you feel trapped? You know what your problem is, Gillian? You can't imagine a relationship that *isn't* a trap."

"You mean they actually exist?"

"There is that possibility."

"You know I feel . . . responsible for you—"

"Bullshit! You're not responsible for anything. I put myself in this chair. It was me who got drunk and decided to try some fancy tricks on a cable car—"

"I remember, Josh—"

"—and you helped me through hell, and I'm grateful, but now my head is back and I accept things the way they are and I don't want pity, especially not from you. If you want to feel trapped, go back to Julian."

As if she'd ever really left him.

Gillian tried to imagine what it would be like, living in Berkeley with a paraplegic lover. ("At least you don't have to worry about me running out on you now," he said shortly after the accident, before the major depression set in. She didn't laugh. She cried. He just watched.) Julian would contest a divorce—he was mean and possessive and liked litigation of all kinds. She might be able to get one of the houses, but then what? The taxes and maintenance would cost a fortune, and despite its notorious success, *Helen Keller in Outer Space* certainly wouldn't cover the costs. Would she give up the Mill Valley Victorian? Could she? She thought of it more as her house than Julian's . . . he was there so little. She had hidden inside a gingerbread fantasy for years, like an overgrown Gretel still fearful of the witch. Josh was right—she *was* spoiled, ruined by the misty Marin mornings, the old, sturdy walls, the spare bedroom she considered her "office"; the antiques and redwood fireplaces, the wallpapers she had collected from all over California. Like so many of her generation, she had taken refuge in a bygone time, casting aside the work and aspirations of postwar parents, flooding back to reinhabit the homes and lives of an earlier generation.

Julian considered Gillian a great asset; the Mill Valley house was a showplace, and Gillian was a perfect hostess. Left to his own devices, Julian would have made a nouveau-riche mess of it. But Gillian had taste. Good taste. Besides, he was so unstable now she couldn't imagine anyone willing to take over her role . . . surely not the masochistic airheads he had taken to trussing and fucking. She had drawn the line firmly at bondage, and Julian had backed off. In their separate bedrooms they achieved a kind of uneasy truce, although Gillian had still not become accustomed to the occasional sight of one of Julian's overnight guests, nude in the kitchen with the indentations of her husband's teeth glowing on her breasts like ringworm. Offering *her* coffee. Gillian. In her own breakfast room.

So. Give it all up? Move into a two-room apartment

off Shattuck with Josh and his wheelchair and his sick
cartoons? Publish the exposé. Pose for *Playboy*. Finish
the cancer novel and sell it to the movies (where the
cancer theme would be excised so quickly as to make
the medical profession gasp). Despite his reputation,
Josh's income was wildly unpredictable. The humor in
his syndicated cartoons was sufficiently unpleasant to
prompt subscriber cancellations (like his answer to
self-appointed book-burners: *Now I Know My ABCs:
An Anti-Intellectual Version.* "A . . . is for shit," it
began.). He had other projects as well. He had designed a brilliant typeface called "Straitjacket" that
was exactly what it sounded like: letterforms created
from the semaphorelike folds of a regulation restraint
camisole. None of the major typeface distributors
would touch it. "A little too psycho-ward," came one of
the responses. "Do you have something that's just
mildly neurotic?"

But Josh didn't do anything mildly. The world was a
psycho ward as far as he was concerned. Gillian loved
his crazy depth-analyses of world and media events, his
wild insights into politics, his obsession with the antibody cults. ("I mean . . . this is even *better* than sex-
change operations . . . incredible material . . . the
transsexuals are reactionary enough in terms of male/
female roles, but the antibodies go them one better—
complete surrender to technological authority.") Josh
was always clipping bizarre little items out of the
newspapers or recording them on videotape. Someone
in San Jose who had grafted audio plugs behind his
ears, then hooked himself into a stereo system, fatally
. . . a successful political candidate, revealed later to be
a functional illiterate . . . a kid in Cupertino who stuck
his hand in a garbage disposal and didn't even flinch.

One of his outstanding obsessions was Venus Tramhell, the rich, maimed sculptress who now presided
over a shadowy underground of performance art. Leg-

endary, though unverifiable, were her "Industrial
Meat" events. The most appalling story in circulation
was that of an evening called "Saturday Night Fetus" in
which actual abortions were animated like puppets on
robot armatures. Whether it was true or not, the story
persisted. Everybody knew somebody who knew somebody who was actually there. Josh had spent quite
some time trying to visualize the spectacle, sketching
the little designer ensembles the fetuses must have
worn, wondering who, exactly, sewed the little costumes (certainly not Venus Tramhell, unless the stories
about her million-dollar mechanical arms were
true . . .).

Josh could laugh at it all, even the stuff that turned
Gillian's stomach. His handicap seemed to sharpen his
powers of observation, and while his observations
were sometimes stranger than reality warranted, Gillian was fascinated by him. "We're really just the
same," he told her. "Just as perverse, just as subversive.
The difference is, you hide behind a pseudonym and
science fiction, and I don't."

But, as Josh observed with increasing frequency,
they *were* living science fiction. And he was probably
right. It was, after all, in science fictional terms that she
dealt with him in her novel. It made more sense, somehow. It was also less painful. During Josh's recupera-
tion, it became apparent that his sexual potency was
not going to return fully. Ever. After numerous consul-
tations, it was suggested that he undergo a prosthetic
implant. A flexible rubber rod would be surgically inserted in the penis, once more enabling normal pene-
tration. At first he refused. Gillian didn't press the
issue. He was a good lover despite his handicap. But
her reassurances didn't help his depression. Finally he
went to the UC Medical Center and had the operation.
When she went to visit him in the hospital, he greeted
her with his usual bizarre humor. "Come on in. Meet

the Bionic Bulge." They laughed then, but afterwards, for a long time, there were tears as well.

Incapacitated and with time on his hands, Josh brooded over the "Industrial Meat" shows to which he never received an invitation ("I'm synthetic from the waist down—doesn't that entitle me?"). The snubs were his own fault. Once he had published a comic book in which Venus Tramhell sat before a mechanical page turner reading *A Farewell to Arms*. Such offenses were not overlooked in the Bay Area's insular and incestuous arts community. Josh's barbs were too raw, too direct. He was always jabbing at the cults, and the cults, it seemed, were now receiving some kind of indirect patronage from Venus Tramhell. She had always been pushing for a machine aesthetic, and now she had a perfect audience.

Josh's interest in cults predated the current nonsense by quite some time. Years before, he had been invited, when it was still in San Francisco, to a People's Temple meeting, but had declined. After Jonestown, it was a decision he regretted, one more proof that he was somehow doomed to live on the sidelines while dark, essential forces that were changing America hovered tantalizingly, just beyond his reach. He became all the more curious about the pathological underside of American culture, the stuff that crawled and wriggled when you picked up the rock. No doubt, Gillian realized, part of his interest in her stemmed from his interest in Julian, a kind of excitement by association. "Only psychopaths can make any difference now," he often said, and Gillian wasn't sure she didn't detect a note of approval in the tone. Approval, and not a little envy.

But Josh was not a psychopath. He had another, private side. The Josh who had affectionate pet names for everything in the house from the salt and pepper shakers to the toilet brush; the Josh who sent out hand-drawn birthday cards to an annual list that must have included two hundred names; the Josh who could do uncanny vocal impressions of just about anybody; the Josh who could make everything into an occasion, an event. If need be, a frozen dinner would be served with a ridiculously expensive wine and eaten to the sound of a rare, out-of-print jazz album he had found while scrounging through the secondhand stores on Telegraph Avenue. ("You *have* to believe me. This is the first time I'm hearing this. I saved it so we could hear it together.") And at times like that Gillian wondered if it were possible that she could ever feel such a surge of longing for another human being. Crazy Josh with his curly hair and red fuzzy beard, trying hard to act demented, but so, so sane . . .

"I got another call," he said, just as Gillian was finishing her coffee.

"You should expect crank calls, given the shots you take at people."

He shook his head. "This is different. There was something really strange. The voice sounded like, you know, one of those gizmos people use when they have their larynx removed."

"What did he say?"

"He? Sounded more like an *it*. Anyway, the gist was that I was being watched."

"Any threats?"

"Nothing direct. Just a complete description of what I did yesterday morning. Where I went, what I was wearing, some trouble I had with the chair. That's the weirdest part. It told me, 'You don't have to have trouble with the chair anymore. We can help you with that.' "

"Help you?"

"Yeah. Help me . . . with a real strange emphasis that even came through over the distortion. I couldn't figure it out."

Gillian stood and pulled on her heavy cotton sweater. "Maybe you should ask some of the people at Independent Living. You know, whether anyone else has been bothered."

He wheeled over and hugged her around the waist. "I'd rather think that it's all for me alone."

"Well, it sounds creepy to me. I'd report it."

"You know what I think they *really* are? Mummies."

"Mummies? You mean like Boris Karloff?"

"Just in a manner of speaking. The Egyptians embalmed their dead to create an impervious physical shell for the afterlife. Can't you see? These 'antibodies' have their own idea of an afterlife, but they do their embalming with machines instead of bandages. And they do it while they're still alive."

"You don't think any of this *works*, do you?"

Josh snorted. "Hell, no. It's all just another New Age scam. Like trance channeling. Like cryogenic coffins."

"But these clinics—apparently they really *are* performing operations."

"Oh, they'll cut you up, all right, the same way a mugger slices you open once he's got your money. And there probably *is* some kind of experimentation going on, but not the kind that's going to give anybody immortality. Nazi stuff. Josef Mengele. A high-tech *Island of Dr. Moreau . . .*" He slipped into a simpering imitation of Peter Lorre.

"And you're just eating it up!"

"A cripple needs a few kicks. You'd rather I was a harmless paraplegic sitting around watching 'Santa Barbara'?"

"What amazes me, Josh, is that I actually consent to spend time with you in the dark."

"But 'cha *do*, Blanche." God. He could even do Bette Davis.

"How can you joke like this? These people could be dangerous."

He snickered. Peter Lorre again. "You think some-body's going to rape me—"

"Josh, stop it. I have to go."

"Can I come to Marin County? Can I, huh? Can I?"

He was begging for a retort. "No dear," she said. "Your wheelchair won't fit in the hot tub."

She was sure the joke would delight him, but the quip fell flat. He let her go and swung around to look out the window. "Maybe it's not the wheelchair that doesn't fit," he said.

THE DOLL HOSPITAL

"Hello, Diandra. My name is Dr. Nagy. Julian Nagy. And you're not going to like me at all."

Diandra lay rigid on the cot, not blinking, not breathing. In point of fact she was both breathing *and* blinking, but she had nearly perfected the illusion of life in total suspension; only a time-lapse camera could record the rise and fall of her breast. The more oxygen you could do without, the better. Just short of asphyxia there was a kind of euphoria, and euphoria was a kind of strength. As for the eyes, she had mastered the trick of blinking at precisely the same moment as the observer. It was an unnerving artifice and an effective one.

The man who called himself Dr. Nagy moved closer. He smelled. It was an acrid stench, like that of someone who hadn't bathed in days. But Diandra didn't really smell him; her sensory processing apparatus *told* her he smelled, and there was a difference. Diandra was beyond primitive feelings like disgust or revulsion. She

81

merely observed the atavistic responses of her now nearly vestigial shell. At a distance. Like a television program. She had seen Nagy on television, heard his hysterical pronouncements. She knew about this place, Resurrection House, and knew that it stood opposed to everything she wanted, everything she had tried to achieve.

No. *Would* achieve.

Nagy leaned closer, and she could see the shaggy stubble of beard that had begun to spread over his face like a fungus. Yes, there was a time when he would have disgusted her, a time when she would have actually recoiled. But there was no room for involuntary physical responses, not now. Not if she was to succeed.

"I know you can hear me, Diandra, so I'll just say what I have to say and then leave. I'm very tired; we've had several new admissions this weekend, and I've been working straight through. I'm tired because I'm a human being, the same way you're a human being, even though you're not about to admit that possibility, at least not at the moment. How you must loathe me! And you know what, Diandra? I approve. I *want* you to loathe me. I want you to *feel*. And I will do anything possible to make you feel. Anything. You might as well know that right now. You don't seem to have a family, and so your employer has entrusted us with your care, and authorized us to do whatever needs to be done.

"So you see, Diandra, you're not going anywhere. We're prepared to have you for a nice long stay. Much nicer, I can assure you, than you would have enjoyed in that place—which clinic was it? Ah, yes, Boca Verde. We'll show you some pictures of what goes on in Boca Verde, by and by. And one day you will thank us for intercepting you and preserving the life you were given.

"There's nothing special about you, Diandra, other than your own unique genetic patterning; nothing superior or outstanding . . . you're just like the rest of us, really. Oh, I know they've taught you differently. But, you came into being through the commingling of genetic material in an act for which there are many euphemisms but which we shall call *fucking*. A cell split, and the resulting cells split again. And again and again until finally *you* were born, squeezed into being through a mess of blood and excrement, a biological fact you can never escape and with which you must come to terms. You will live out your life in a biological envelope, and you will die in it as well. There is no escape. Not through the Cybernetic Temple, not anywhere.

"You have been brainwashed, Diandra. You are a prisoner of war, a hostage who has come to identify with her captors, even to protect them. We will show you that you are wrong. We will take what time it takes. You came in here believing you are a machine, but you will leave here knowing that you are a woman.

"On the other hand, perhaps you won't leave at all."

Diandra watched the face recede. She watched the strange grin play about the lips; a cruel, peculiar fixity. He moved toward the door. A woman in an institutional uniform waited just outside, standing watch. She was stiff and cool and stood motionless during Nagy's harangue. Stoic, mechanical . . . Diandra found her far more agreeable than the sweating, leering doctor. Perhaps she could make an ally—

"You'll have to get used to a few new things," the doctor continued wearily. "You'll have to start eating normal food again, and drinking normal water. You will probably experience some withdrawal, and it won't be pleasant. Yes, you've been drugged as well. So I suggest you start changing your attitude right now. It will really help. Don't think of this as a prison, or a punishment. Think of it as . . . a doll hospital. Yes, a place for broken playthings to get fixed up right. Where Pinocchio gets to be a real live boy. The place where toys become real.

"And, in the likely event that you keep resisting our help, we've even provided you with a mechanical friend whom you may trust more than us. Yes, it's a computer. It can talk to you and you can talk back. You just type whatever you want and it appears on the screen. No tricks, no real people. Completely artificial. You'll be right at home.

"Now, I'm exhausted and I'm going to say good night. We'll start work tomorrow." He turned to leave, then stopped. "Oh. One more thing. I'm on to that blinking trick, so you really don't have to waste any more energy trying to impress me."

" 'Night, Doll," said the woman in the uniform. The heavy door slammed shut.

Diandra closed her eyes and tried to will herself out of her body, out of the room, out of Resurrection House and into the higher plane the Temple had promised her. A dimension of higher, finer frequencies . . . she deserved it and it deserved her. But she wasn't ready, hadn't finished the preparations. In Boca Verde, in the jungle clinic, they would have made the first structural alterations. It was going to be a new beginning. It was destined to be. *They promised*.

She stopped struggling with her body momentarily, and her breathing returned to normal, or at least what *they* considered normal. He had talked about drugs in her food. What about the poisons in the air, the insidious biological hazards that were everywhere, in everything? Escaping the body was the only real escape, finally. They said Philip had signed the papers, ordered her locked up. Where was he now? Being fed a lot of lies, most likely.

Diandra let her mind blot out the room and let the memories of her gradual induction into the Temple play themselves back to her, as if on a screen. Perhaps she could find a clue . . .

After the night with Venus Tramhell her life had
taken on an increasingly dreamlike quality. "Let yourself go," the older woman had coaxed her. "Let your
body go." The videotape always left her in a curious,
half-numb state. She remembered Venus, straddling her
like a mantis; the mechanical arms were like something
out of a half-remembered midnight movie. Their motors purred contentedly as the rubber-tipped swivel
fingers kneaded her flesh. "Where did you . . . ?" Diandra began to ask, but Venus hushed her. "You might say
they were a gift. From a wealthy admirer." The rubber
tips began to vibrate, as if in response to a silent myo-
electrical command from Venus's brain. Diandra
gasped as the appliances reached her pubis.

". . . yourself go—"

"Yes—"

"You don't have any idea of how good it can be—"

"D-don't stop—"

Venus didn't stop. And neither did Diandra.

Afterwards, when Venus had put away her "toys," as
she called them, she stood before the massive platform
bed and stared at Diandra coldly. "I'm sending you
home now. I find sleep disgusting, but they haven't
found a way around it yet. It's not something I do with
people. In front of people."

"I . . . understand." She stared blankly at the stainless
steel industrial frieze that loomed over the bed.

"No you don't. Not yet."

"I want to see you again."

"Oh, you will. And with luck you'll see beyond me.
Through me. You'll see things you never dreamed.
From the minute I saw your windows at Croesus I
knew I would be able to share my vision with you,
whoever you were . . . and whatever you might
become."

A few weeks later Diandra began to receive video-
tapes in the mail. There was no return address, but she
assumed that Venus had something to do with it. They

arrived in seamless plastic mailing bags with her name computer-printed on the label. Like the first one, they were powerfully hypnotic and arresting. The images were alternately strange and soothing . . . scenes of disease and decay juxtaposed with the most advanced medical technology. The voice spoke English, but the accent was electronic.

". . . to begin Lecture Number Three on the evolution of human consciousness. When last we met, we left the human race on the brink of its next major evolutionary step, a step as profound as the first amphibious organism heaving itself onto dry land. But organism has now reached the limits of its potential. And that is why *organism* created *mechanism*. . . ."

Diandra listened, rapt. She had never heard such a voice before: authoritative, resonant, something neither male nor female, beyond the flesh. The pulsating light, too, was entrancing. She could stare at that light forever.

". . . those of you who have been chosen to hear this message are special . . . each in your own way has some special quality that has earned you the privilege. Think of yourself as a pioneer, venturing into uncharted lands that will forever alter the course of human destiny. Many of you have felt isolated in your present lives, alienated from your peers. But, of course! You *are* different. You *are* special. And now the time has come for your natural superiority to assert itself and be rewarded. . . ."

The voice went on and on. The world was due for change—radical change. It would be a long, difficult struggle to gain acceptance, but inevitably, *their* view of "life" would prevail. The United States government in collusion with the medical establishment was deliberately withholding information on certain breakthroughs. Artificial replacements for vital organs . . . myoelectric prostheses . . . biocompatible silicon rubber . . . fluorocarbon substitutes for blood itself. Certain elective procedures were now possible that could indefinitely extend the human life span. Virtual immortality might be at hand.

"Unfortunately, nearly all these procedures are still considered illegal in this country, despite the recent widespread deregulation of our health care system. More deregulation is required, not just in medicine but in all matters of trade and free choice. America's laissez-faire dream has yet to be realized. If we cannot make decisions as basic as the control and disposal of our own bodies, then we cannot truly be considered free.

"It will take a long, hard effort to reverse public opinion and policy. There will be confrontations. There may even be violence. Fund-raising is especially crucial, and special instructions will reach you concerning the most effective means of soliciting contributions. And your hard work will be rewarded. A limited number of you will be accepted into special programs outside the country, where pioneering medical procedures will be—in fact, *are being*—carried out, free from prying eyes.

"Remember—those who commit now have the greatest chance of escaping the cancers, the disease, the inevitable degeneration that most Americans will face. You deserve more. You've earned it. You've worked hard, you've paid your taxes, and what have you received in return? Lies. Betrayal. A sentence of death. After all, what do you have to look forward to? A few years of enforced 'retirement' in a burnt-out shell of a 'body,' and then—oblivion.

"It needn't be this way. And it won't be, if you plan now. For a limited time, qualified individuals may elect to be part of one of the greatest revolutions in medicine. Artificial organ replacements, cybernetic augmentation . . . all can help you to retain your vitality indefinitely and help you achieve your higher potential.

"As I mentioned, special procedures are currently being carried out in Central and South American compounds until the technicalities of domestic licensing are complete. But we wanted you to be among the first to know of these amazing discoveries and their possible availability to you. Unfortunately, the operations are expensive, and not everyone can be accepted. A lottery may be required. But the details will be dealt with. The important thing to remember is that *there is hope*. 'Life,' as you have been taught to accept it, need not be the end, but merely a beginning."

The tapes had another, odd effect on Diandra, beyond their overt substantive content. One afternoon, for instance, she felt herself compelled to stop in at the public library to look up a medical publication, *The Journal of Artificial Organ Research*. She had never heard of the periodical, and yet seemed to know exactly where to find it. It was as if she had received the instruction subliminally. Perhaps she had. But her trust in the tapes was so complete that she was not disturbed in the least. She leafed through the magazines, absorbing the words and images like a sponge soaking up a chemical spill. It seemed that there was not a single part of the human body that some researcher, somewhere, was not attempting to replace. There were artificial joints, artificial hearts, artificial skin, and artificial blood. There were arteries made of Dacron, silicon breasts and testicles, plans for plastic windpipes, a rubber larynx, hearing aids that doubled as radio receivers. She found pictures of prototypes for artificial lungs—plastic bags filled with coils of Teflon; she perused proposals for implantable artificial kidneys and various devices for direct electrical stimulation of the brain.

She left the library breathless, dizzy, and not a little exhilarated.

One afternoon the following week Philip stopped by her office. "I wondered if you were planning to take in the automaton exhibit at the City Museum. There's got to be some material for you there."

"I'm way ahead of you, Philip. In fact, I was just leaving to go there now."

Philip smiled. "I shouldn't have assumed something like that would escape your notice. See you later, then. Enjoy." He turned to leave, but stopped upon seeing a photograph tacked to Diandra's gridlike bulletin board.

"Very cute. Anybody I should know?"

"It's Robert Jarvik," said Diandra absently, zipping her bag. "He invented the artificial heart, remember?"

"I shouldn't have asked," said Philip, with feigned rejection.

"I thought you were sublimating these days."

"If you want to call it that."

"I read about those safe-sex machines they've introduced in Japan. Maybe we could get one on loan for the new installation—"

"Enough, Diandra. Even Croesus has limits."

"Not if profits are involved."

"*Goodbye*, Diandra. Enjoy the museum."

Diandra hailed a cab outside the St. Francis Hotel for the short trip to the Civic Center. The City Museum was a new, flexible space that specialized in unpredictable exhibits. So far, it had lived up to its reputation. The new attraction was an ambitious display of antique automata from all over the world. Recreating human life in mechanical simulacra was as old as watchmaking, it seemed; it was no wonder that some of the most splendid examples on display were Swiss. Diandra picked up an exhibit catalog and began to move among the ticking, life-sized figures. The aural effect was that of wandering through an existential clock factory where the hour never struck. The robots were dressed in period costumes and performed simple, repetitive tasks; a child copied out letters in an impeccable hand, stopping regularly to fill its pen and blot the paper. A monk said a perfect rosary, bead by bead, and while no voice remained (an ancient bellows within was beyond repair), Diandra could almost read the lips of the mannequin. *Hail Mary, full of grace.* She moved on quickly to the next specimen. A young woman played a real harpsichord; an uncomplicated arrangement of a familiar Mozart piece. Her back was completely open to view, revealing the intricate machinery and player-piano type of mechanism that programmed her performance. No electronics, no microchips. All this, two hundred years before Disney.

She had a sudden sensation of *déjà vu*, which gave way to an actual memory: a field trip the nuns had organized, so many years before, to an exhibit at the Cleveland Museum of Health. Diandra and the other children had been herded into a room to see "Juno, the Transparent Woman." Juno had been molded of plastic and glass, her hands extended palms upward as if to display the stigmata. Her "voice" had boomed authoritatively from a loudspeaker as she gave the assembled a guided tour of her anatomy, each organ lighting up in response to an audio cue. Heart. Lungs. Ovaries. *This is my body.* The museum had smelled of disinfectant. Diandra remembered pressing to the front, clutching the cool railing that separated the android from its audience. The nuns had had to nearly pry her away.

Now, the new displays reminded her of the sisters: a fortune-telling witch from a 1920s amusement park or penny arcade. A basket of metal slugs was provided for visitors to activate the figure. Behind scratched, dusty glass, the old woman leaned slightly forward, head bowed. The effect was startling enough in its dormant mode; the detailing on the hair and hands was the work of a true artisan. Or a mortician, Diandra thought. Impulsively, she inserted a counterfeit coin. The machinery whirred. The old woman raised her head. The eyes cracked open, the lids pulled back in wrinkled bunches like miniature Austrian drapes. The glass eyes scanned her through the imperfect, distorting glass. A crabbed hand levitated, reaching to choose a card. *The Ace of Spades. It has to be the death card*, Diandra thought. Correctly.

The crone slumped forward into mechanical oblivion.

"Excuse me," came a voice behind her. Startled, she turned. A thin man with dark glasses faced her. He wore some kind of industrial jumpsuit. His hair was limp and prematurely grey.

"Yes?"

"You're Diandra, aren't you?"

"Who—"

"Venus. I'm sorry, I'm a friend of Venus. She said I should meet you."

Diandra was wary. "Have you been following me?"

"No, not really. I stopped by your office. Philip recognized me from one of the parties. He said I might find you here."

"It's a fascinating exhibit."

"Like your displays. At Croesus."

Diandra stared at him. This wasn't a pickup. And he wasn't gay, either. "What do you want?"

"To talk. I . . . I have something for you. To tell you and show you. The museum has a cafeteria, I think, just downstairs."

If Venus says so . . .

"All right," said Diandra. The cafeteria was all neon and leopard skin, the "Memphis" style Diandra detested. She tried to focus past it. Who was this creature? He was emaciated, sexless. But earnest. Very earnest.

Diandra took coffee, and the nameless man paid the minimum for a cup of hot water. They sat at a lacquered table in the far corner of the room. "I'm Robbie," he said, emptying some silver-grey powder from an envelope into his cup. Diandra didn't comment. "You'd probably be surprised at how many fans you have in town. There are really quite a few of us. We can't wait to see what you're going to do next." Diandra thought of the crowds she sometimes saw, pressing against the Union Square windows. People with more than just casual interest . . .

"Well, you may have to start paying admission soon. The installations draw the customers, but they're getting expensive."

"Admission? You're kidding."

"Not at all. Shopping is a form of entertainment, and there's no reason it should be given away free. They'll pay. You'll see." She was starting to sound like Philip, she realized.

"Well, I hope I can afford the privilege. I don't know anything about entertainment, but I do know that what you do is a kind of performance art."

"Thank you. You're very kind."

"No, I'm not kind. I don't really have any feelings at all."

It was then that Diandra recognized Robbie as a kind of octave variation on Andy Warhol. The dead Andy Warhol.

"You felt the need to talk to me."

"I guess I *try* not to have feelings. But we were grateful to hear that you were . . . one of us."

"Us?"

"Like I said, you have a lot of fans." He took a sip of the strange, chalky-looking drink he had mixed. Then he slipped off his dark glasses.

And Diandra saw.

Saw what Robbie could not see, not with his left eye, at least. Because he had no left eye. Instead, there was something that looked like the lens of a camera.

"It doesn't work, at least not anymore. I was blinded in a stupid car wreck, about ten years ago. They couldn't save the eye at all. So I volunteered for an experiment in artificial sight restoration. The camera is, or was, hooked up to an electrode plate that was implanted on the surface of the visual cortex." He leaned forward and parted a thin patch of hair. Diandra could see the scar on the back of his cranium.

"We actually made quite a bit of progress. First they just stimulated the cortex directly. And I could see! Simple shapes at first—squares, circles, arrows. They could even control the colors a bit. Then it *really* got interesting when I let them put in the camera and the plate. We got to the point where, through my left eye, the world looked like a computer billboard, which is exactly how it worked. Eventually, the resolution would be improved to that of a color TV monitor—in other words, almost perfect natural vision.

"But in the meantime, I had this fabulous experience of seeing normally through one eye, but at the same time seeing this whole *digital* reality superimposed by the other one. I mean, I could have sold it to MTV! It was incredible, really incredible."

"What . . . happened?" asked Diandra.

Robbie's expression turned sour. "They *said* their funding ran out, but that wasn't the whole story. They didn't like me. I was too enthusiastic about the whole thing, not just some complacent guinea pig. So they pulled the plug. I was on the verge of this . . . this . . . *vision*, I mean a really significant psycho-cybernetic breakthrough, and they pulled the goddamn plug."

"So that's why you're interested in the Temple?"

"You bet I'm interested! The government is trying to hide the facts—*but the technology is available*. Not here, but in Latin America for sure, and I think there are some clinics in Switzerland and Denmark. Places where they're not afraid to see this thing through to the end. That's what we're working for now. To raise money for the clinics, the research. And, of course, we want to go ourselves. And if things become too repressive here . . . "

"Repressive?"

"Hell, they act like they own us. We essentially have no control over our bodies. They're trying to squash us, especially those of us who've had a taste of what's possible. They want to limit our potential, keep hidden the facts about organ replacement. About the real possibility of human immortality in our lifetime. And those of us who are ready for it—and I'm convinced that some of us have been ready for it since birth—well, we're not going to wait much longer."

"What will you do?"

"Eventually, I'm going to have this thing fixed up right. Then I'll probably have the other one taken out, too. And then—"

"Excuse me," said Diandra, rising. "I really have to—"

"No, please. I mean, I'm sorry, I know I can get carried away. I didn't mean to upset you." He fumbled in his jumpsuit's several pockets. "Here. I wanted you to have this. All of us read it." He handed her a paperback book. Diandra glanced at the cover. There was a painting superimposing a spaceship over a brain, with two disembodied eyes staring directly at you from a laminated void.

The title of the book was *Helen Keller in Outer Space*.

"You'll really like it. I'm surprised Venus didn't already recommend it. You'll read it, won't you?"

"Well, yes, I suppose so." *If Venus says so.*

When Diandra looked up from the book, Robbie was gone. Why had the image transfixed her so? And why had Robbie been so quick to disappear? Not that she had been particularly comfortable with him. She slipped the book into her bag and left the museum. But as she left, she caught a glimpse of the grey, metallic sludge he had left at the bottom of his coffee cup and wondered what on earth he had been drinking.

That night, she read *Helen Keller in Outer Space* in a single sitting. She lost all track of time; it was nearly three in the morning when she finished. The story had transfixed her. Spaceships were powered by disembodied human brains grafted into computers. A woman doctor, a telepathic psychiatrist, had the job of "breaking through" to the brain of a disabled catatonic ship. What resulted was the strangest and most compelling love story she had ever experienced. The doctor becomes infatuated with a bodiless man and finally sacrifices her own body to be with him. It was all irresistibly romantic, and Diandra knew she would return to it again and again. She noted that the novel had been through several printings and was regarded as the "bible" of the antibody subculture, although the author was some kind of recluse who disavowed any link to the movement.

The following afternoon, she received a phone call from Venus Tramhell. Her heart skipped a beat at the sound of her dark contralto.

"Diandra, darling. I wondered if you're free tonight. I'm hosting a little soirée and thought you might find it interesting. There'll be a lot of people. At least, nominally people. I really don't think you should miss it."

She thought of Venus's prosthetic arms bringing her to orgasm with a powerful mingling of nausea and yearning. But mostly yearning.

"Well . . . yes. I'd like that very much."

"Good. It won't be at my house. I try to keep the location of these events secret. Too many gate crashers otherwise. You'll understand why. My car will come by about midnight, if that's all right."

"Fine. I'll be waiting."

"I've missed seeing you, Diandra. I hope you feel the same. Something very special happened between us. A certain . . . electricity, wouldn't you say?"

Diandra didn't say. Venus didn't seem to take offense. "See you at midnight," she said.

•

A stretch limo appeared before Diandra's Pacific Avenue apartment house exactly at twelve. The back door opened by itself. Inside, Diandra could see Venus depressing a foot pedal. She was wearing one of the Halston gowns, a silk turban, and, as a final touch, unsettling to even Diandra, a colorful profusion of party streamers cascading from each creamy stump.

"Diandra, you're dressed so conservatively! It's Halloween. Have you forgotten?"

"I . . . guess so. I'm sorry."

"Not to worry, dear. You look fine. Now, get in."

Diandra slid into the huge back compartment. Venus stepped on the pedal, and the door slammed and locked. Venus leaned close, and Diandra could smell her delicately metallic cologne. "I'd love to give you a hug, Diandra, but my playthings are very delicate, and I can't take them out. Later, perhaps."

The driver took them south of Market, to the Folsom Street area, where they arrived at an unmarked warehouse. The streets seemed deserted, save for a few burly men in full leather moving furtively in the shadows and doorways. "It's getting difficult to keep finding new locations. We don't want any infiltrators. So far, we've been fortunate." The driver signaled to one of the leathermen who unroped a parking spot for them near the warehouse entrance. The driver helped Venus from the compartment. He ignored Diandra entirely.

Inside, the amplified music by Philip Glass was nearly deafening. The party was in full swing, but the crowd parted at the entrance of Venus. She glided to the center of the room, a commanding presence, her streamers trailing behind her like psychedelic comet tails.

There was applause. "Venus, Venus," they chanted, in perfect synchronization with *Einstein on the Beach*. Venus revolved, seeking out the spotlight. She found it quickly, and Diandra watched the masked revelers flood the space around her. She reached out with her stumps to embrace someone in a futuristic costume . . . Diandra had the strange, giddy feeling that many of those present might not be in costume at all. There were androids and robots, a woman with an exterior circulatory system pumping glowing fluids through transparent veins that covered her like a veil of vermicelli. Silver contact lenses, fiber-optic manes of hair . . . men and women, nearly nude, completely shaved, and painted with metallic body makeup. Many, she realized, had imitated her own window displays. They were very well done; closely observed, probably from photographs. There were numerous amputees in attendance, some with elaborate, souped-up prostheses, but nothing, of course, that compared to Venus's remarkable components. She wondered about the people with the missing limbs. Wondered if their conditions had occurred through accident. Or design.

"Hello, Diandra. I had a feeling you'd be here."

She turned to stare into Robbie's dead electronic eye. For some reason, at first, it didn't occur to her to look at the other. "You disappeared so quickly the other day. I couldn't thank you for the book."

"I had a feeling you'd read it right away. Remarkable, isn't it?"

"Yes. I think we could work a window around it. It's really quite . . . compelling." She noticed Robbie's bulky costume, 1950s retro-tech.

"Do you like it? I'm Robbie the Robot tonight. And who knows—maybe tomorrow, too." He turned and clanked away.

"Robbie told me who you are," said a girl at her side.

Her head was shaved in a Mohawk shaped like a lightning bolt, and she wore form-fitting sunglasses that
gave the impression of being fused into her skull. "You
practically have your own cult. That window of the
housewife, you know, with a blender for a head and
eggbeaters for hands—wow!" She took a sip of something from a plastic cup. Diandra saw that it was the
same grey sludge that Robbie had mixed for himself in
the museum cafeteria. "I'm glad you finally showed up.
I'm one to talk—it took *me* long enough to get involved. I tried a lot of things—scientology, Ayn Rand . . .
cripe, I must have read *Atlas Shrugged* fifteen times.
The problem was, all it did was just let you *feel* superior. You couldn't *do* anything with it. But this is
different."

"What do you . . . do?"

"Not much—yet. I'm still in Stage One. I'm on the
diet—this stuff is about all I eat anymore. It's completely nonorganic. Cleans you out. Stops your periods.
Gets you ready for the big stuff. Want a taste?"

"No—not right now. Thanks."

The girl smiled and took another sip. "Venus brought
you here. You're lucky, having a sponsor like her."

"She's a remarkable woman."

"What's left of the woman. I can't wait to see what
she's like when they finish the renovations."

"Renovations?"

"She didn't tell you? Well, I guess a lot of it is just
gossip, but the word is, she's going to have *everything*
replaced. Total prosthesis. And you know, it's really
important. We *need* role models."

The girl didn't seem to mind when Diandra drifted
away into the crowd. She caught glimpses of Venus as
she was feted by the adoring mob. A bank of television
monitors floated above the dance floor, a visual com-
plement to the synthetic music. Computer animation,
some of it surrealistic, some of it startlingly naturalis-

tic. When an oddly familiar face appeared at an anchor desk, silently reading a news report, Diandra wondered why she couldn't place the face—

"Amazing, isn't it?" said a passing android, noticing her interest. "Completely digital. They took tapes of the three network anchors and, well, just connected the dots. This one would get better ratings than all three combined. Here. This is for you." Diandra found a stapled sheaf of papers thrust into her hands. Photocopied articles from the scientific and popular press. New advances in artificial organ research. Dot-matrix diatribes on various "cover-ups" . . . if all these breakthroughs had been cleared for public consumption, how much more had been accomplished in government *secrecy*? There were lists of certain doctors "sympathetic" to the antibody plight, details on computer information networks. As she flipped through the sheets the words NO MORE BACK ALLEY AMPUTATIONS leapt from the page and into her brain.

Less is more . . . the next evolutionary step . . . casting off the protoplasmic coil . . . inevitable. . . .

"Could I have a taste of that?" she asked the bartender tentatively. He smiled behind a memory-board mask and poured her the grey fluid from a laboratory flask. "Thank you," she said quietly. The taste was chalky. After a while she got used to it. No one was actually dancing, she realized, although in some anthropological sense it could be considered a dance. They were making connections. Networking. The music pounded. *So this is my audience.* She set down her empty cup and headed for the lavatory. She felt dizzy, not quite right. What was in that drink? It wasn't alcohol, that was for sure. The women's room was crowded when she entered. Several masked women were gathered around a stall. Cocaine? One of the women beckoned to her. She looked over her shoulder, to be sure she wasn't indicating someone else, and it was then that she saw the wrecked tampon dispenser with the words NEVER AGAIN slashed across the wall.

Slowly, Diandra approached the stall. There was a heavy, rhythmic splashing sound. A firm hand gloved in rubber grasped her shoulder and pulled her forward. The two innermost figures knelt before the basin. They had inserted intravenous needles into the crooks of their thin arms. The needles were attached to open-ended catheters that spat blood against porcelain. They were chanting something, *sotto voce*. When one of them started to swoon, one of the standing members took charge. "That's enough for you two." She poured in some industrial disinfectant, pressed the flush handle, and the blood was swallowed in a roar of water.

"*That's* what toilets are for," the woman said, turning to face Diandra. The image of Reddy Kilowatt had been tattooed to her brow. "Okay, honey—how about you?"

Diandra bolted.

Outside, the cavernous dance space was filled with the sounds of *Glassworks*. Venus was nowhere in sight. Near the bar she thought she saw an "android" peeling open a package of batteries, the small, round kind used in cameras and watches. He popped one into his mouth and offered the other to a friend. Candy. Diandra propelled herself in another direction, attracted by the crowd that gathered at the entrance to a smaller, back room. The music was different. Disco. And there was a peculiar chemical smell in the air. Formaldehyde?

"Diandra. I'm so glad I found you." She felt Venus's stump caress her cheek. "I was so afraid you'd miss the highlight of the evening. Our *pièce de résistance*."

Diandra stiffened. "I'm . . . really not feeling well. I think I ought to leave."

"Nonsense. The back room is especially for you tonight." She felt Venus's body pressed against hers like a steel buttress. She steered her toward the room. The crowd parted. She could see more now, and the music

ELTING MEMORIAL LIBRARY
93 Main Street
New Paltz, New York 12561

was louder. She heard the sound of strange machinery. A low-slung light cast shadows up on the walls, magnified shadows of tiny human figures with oversized heads, like rubbery marionettes in the hands of a mechanical Gepetto . . .

"No—I won't!"

"Diandra! This is in your honor. You're going to look—"

"One of us!" shouted a voice from the shadows.

Diandra pulled away from Venus's feeble grasp. "Stop her!" she cried to a pair of flunkies. The androids *manqué* held Diandra by either arm. Venus hissed in her ear. "Don't you understand—this is a tribute to you! It's only a puppet show, for God's sake—"

Puppets? The formaldehyde stench stung her nostrils. The dancing fetal shadows loomed above her like hydrocephalic nightmares.

The music was "Staying Alive."

"Take her to the table. She'll look, I tell you!"

"*Let me go!*" Diandra screamed. And then she underscored the demand the only way she possibly could.

She stuck a finger down her throat and vomited. Directly into the faces of her captors, first one and then the other. Heaved up her guts on their painted silver faces. They released her instantly, shrieking. As Diandra guessed, body fluids were as effective a repellent as tear gas. Or wolfsbane. They crawled off into the darkness tearing at their soiled costumes, spitting out the puke that had dribbled into their mouths. The other antibodies recoiled as well, spreading out in a ragged circle from Venus and Diandra. The music had stopped. The disco lights flickered around them silently, like motorized fireflies. Diandra wiped her mouth and stared at Venus in her turban and her gown, the streamers hanging from her stumps like ugly nerve endings in the night.

"You . . . animal," Venus said.

"And what about you? *You're* still half meat. I

wouldn't be calling names. You don't think I haven't
seen you sneaking solid food?" The image of Venus,
alone in her sterile kitchen, draped with a veil as she
bent over a plate—

The antibodies gasped at Diandra's impertinence.
But Venus only smiled. "You *are* stronger than I
thought. But I can deal with that, too. At home."

"I don't want—"

"You don't *know* what you want, Diandra. I do.
That's your problem, and my advantage." She turned to
one of her pale sycophants. "I want you to see that the
installation is completely destroyed before morning.
Do you understand? *Completely*. And I apologize to
everyone for our guest's lack of manners. Too *much*
breeding, I suppose."

•

The ride back up into Pacific Heights was completed
in silence. At the crest of Divisadero, scudding fog
toyed with the gables of Venus's Victorian manse. The
driver helped Venus out of the car and, as earlier, ignored Diandra. But she wasn't thinking about him. Her
head was still swimming with that strange drink. After
everything that happened, why had Venus asked her
back? And, more important, why had she come?

Diandra followed Venus to her bedchamber.

"Help me with my earrings," she commanded, and
Diandra obeyed. "You have a lot to learn. More than I
thought."

Diandra dropped the earrings into the lab tray on
Venus's high-tech dressing table. Venus shook off her
turban. Her silver-shot hair cascaded to her shoulders.
She bit off the party streamers and spat them on the
floor. "Why did you do it? You, of all people. They
adored you. They're your audience, your public—"

"I don't think about 'my public.' I just want to do my
work."

"In that department store? That's a laugh. Oh, it's

entertaining enough . . . it certainly caught *my* attention. But you're being wasted there. You should be at the cutting edge of your art, the way I was at mine. Do you have any idea of the influence you could have?"

"Or do you mean the influence *you* could have through me?"

"Admit it, Diandra. There was nothing in that back room that you haven't dreamed of doing. Admit it."

Diandra said nothing, but she thought of the many sketches, beginning with the robot madonna, that had disturbed her so much that she had to destroy them. It was true. There was nothing in that back room that she couldn't imagine herself. Or hadn't.

"In the lavatory there were women . . . bleeding themselves." It wasn't like that in *Helen Keller in Outer Space*.

"So what? They have to start somewhere. You started yourself, in New York. With the hysterectomy—"

"I needed it!" she lied.

"You *wanted* it. There's a difference. I'm not going to let you hang back with the apes, Diandra. Here. I'll fix you a drink." She pressed a foot pedal at the automated wet bar. Grey fluid filled a fluted glass.

"I don't think I want any—"

"Drink it," said Venus as she went into her dressing room. "It will help you understand."

Diandra gripped the glass by the stem. What did Venus want from her, anyway? To be her arms? She took a long pull at the quicksilver cocktail. She looked around the room. The industrial slab of a bed, the severe decor, the modern vertical blinds in the Victorian window bay. And the foot pedals. Everywhere, the goddamn foot pedals . . .

"Happy Halloween, Diandra."

She turned to see Venus in the door of her dressing room. She was nude, her body pale and shaved. She seemed to be wearing a pair of folded umbrellas, one on each abbreviated arm. She moved to the window bay and there let unfurl what Diandra could only imagine to be a computer's conception of the wings of a bat or a pterodactyl. A thin synthetic membrane was stretched tight over the mechanical frame, and Diandra could see the pneumatic hinges and veinlike wiring that crawled beneath the translucent skin. At the farthest extensions were a matching pair of three-fingered robotic arms that beckoned, beckoned . . .

"Another gift from a wealthy admirer. An indulgence for a special occasion."

Diandra drifted to the window bay. The prosthesis matched the color of Venus's pale skin exactly; it was impossible to tell where the "woman" ended and the "costume" began. The wings encircled her. Robot hands undressed her. Venus thrust her hairless pudenda against Diandra's groin, and she could feel the unmistakable sensation of a vibrator. But this vibrator was buried in the flesh of the user. "Do you like it? I had it implanted a few weeks ago . . . completely electrostimulating . . . " Diandra responded, felt the yearning swell within her. "And it's only the beginning, Diandra. Eventually, they'll be able to bypass the nervous system completely. I didn't really think about it until I lost my arms, but then it hit me. That it's all in the brain, finally. Pain, pleasure, experience. Soon they'll be able to go into the cortex directly . . . there'll be biocompatible computer chips . . . brain-to-brain hookups . . . memory transferred to indestructible holographic plates . . . "

They moved to the bed. Venus grasped her in the scissors position. The vibrator purred in its burrow of flesh. The mechanical wings beat softly against the parachute fabric that covered the pallet, a delicate sound. In a way, the bionic cocoon reminded her of the flapping raiment of the nuns who taught her. If wine could be turned into blood, then couldn't blood be turned into something else?

"And once the body is disposed of, there will be only complete knowledge and infinite consciousness . . . "

"Yes—"

"Infinite pleasure—"

"Oh, God—"

"And life everlasting . . ."

Diandra felt the climaxes begin, wave after wave, building and building—

"That . . . that would be . . ."

"Yes . . . ?"

". . . would be . . ."

"Go on—"

"*Heaven*!"

Diandra crested.

And the wings of the Machine God engulfed her.

BETTER THINGS
FOR BETTER LIVING

"Excuse me . . . ?"

"Yes, Miss?"

"I was wondering if you could give me some information about organ donations."

"Why, yes, of course. You'd like a donor card."

"Well, yes . . . I mean, no. I mean, I'd like to *be* a donor."

"Then the first step is the card—"

"No . . . I . . . you . . . don't understand. I already know the donation I want to make. It's not for the future. I know now. Specifically."

"Oh, I understand, it's a *family* member. A kidney—"

"No. Not a family member. And not a kidney."

"Then what—"

"A heart transplant. I want to be a donor for a heart transplant."

"Miss, what are you talking about?"

"You do heart transplants here, and the mechanical thing, too. It's in the papers all the time, it's not a secret—"

"Please, lower your voice—"

"I read all about it, how difficult it is to get donors for the transplants. How the artificial heart patients aren't strong enough. I'm here to offer an exchange; it's as simple as that."

"You're obviously upset—"

"I get what I want, and you get what you want—"

"Miss, this is a public area, I have to ask you to—"

"Is anything wrong here?"

"You—are you a doctor? Are you in charge? In control? I have something to show you—"

"I . . . think it would be better if we talked someplace else—"

"Good . . . I have all the proof I need. Things you need to know. Then it will all make sense. Is this your office, your desk? Look, here in my bag, let me spread them out—"

"What exactly are these?"

"They're letters. Responses to a classified ad I took out in a newspaper a few weeks ago. Look—you know how many there are here? Hundreds! I got the idea from a Phil Donahue show on surrogate mothers . . . except it wasn't my uterus I was offering. And you know what? They're willing to *pay*—God, how they're willing to pay! Rich people with heart problems. They're afraid of the mechanical thing but can't find donors. Rich people! Wanting to pay *me!* And I didn't even ask for money—"

"Selling organs . . . that's illegal—"

"Oh, sure, for now. But they'll deregulate it just like everything else, in time."

"But . . . why would you want to go through with such a thing?"

"Because I can. Because it can finally be done. Because people like you need people like me."

"Yes . . . I think I've read about 'people like you.' Even seen you, clustered outside the hospital anytime we're implanting a mechanical heart . . ."

"We always make a point of . . . being near."

"And you really want . . . you really believe . . . ?"

"It's not a matter of belief. It's a matter of what I know. I may have been born meat, but I don't have to die that way. Admit it, Doctor. I'm just what you've always wanted."

"What you're proposing is preposterous—"

"Is it? I don't think so. Oh, you'll go through all the rituals, your boards of review, all that bureaucratic shit. But in the end, you'll rationalize it and you'll give me a call. This is a profit-making hospital; they're not charities anymore. And your heart business is suffering from a lack of healthy donors. You can't deny it."

"You may be physically healthy—"

"But you doubt my sanity?"

"Frankly, yes. The psychological condition of any donor or recipient is crucial. Even if what you're proposing were in the realm of possibility, and I'm *not* saying that it is, there would be a great deal of preoperative counseling and evaluation. Like the transsexual procedure—"

"Fuck it. I'm sick of being compared to sex-changers all the time! *They're* just trading off one disease for another. I'm talking about something else. The start of the next evolutionary step—"

"I see."

"No you don't. But you will, believe me. They do these things in Mexico already, but I don't trust them. I want it public. I want it here. Made in America. I want to make a statement, good PR, not some sleazy backstreet amputation—"

"Amputation? I thought we were talking about transplants. Implants."

"You don't think we want to stop at one organ? What would be the point? The long-range goal is total prosthesis. I know you people are interested in other things, too—nerve grafts, artificial limbs, the works. There's a lot of money in it. But you can't make any money if you have to keep waiting for the right kind of accidents to happen."

"Your body isn't a . . . garage sale."

"I told you before. I'm not selling. I'm giving. And sooner or later, *you're* going to be on the take. So why not get in at the ground level?"

"I think you're a very disturbed young woman."

"Good. That shows you're thinking about me, and that's the first step. Now just keep thinking. About your career. About the future. About where we're all inevitably heading. And when the pressure from your stockholders becomes sufficiently intense, and all the obstacles have been rationalized away . . . well, you have my card, there on your desk. Doctor? Is there anything wrong? Anything I can . . . do?"

MEDIA MACHINATIONS

You spread open the magazine on your desk blotter, just as you earlier spread the Silicon Valley Housewife. The blotter paper still holds the odor of her musk, the scent of your conquest. But the control of one confused woman is nothing compared to the potential control of millions of minds through the technology of the mass media. You have purchased this magazine with more than passing interest. A colorful, cartoonish newsweekly, it has given over several editorial pages to the subject of your obsession. A bold, two-page headline sets the tone:

UN-PEOPLE? NEW CULTS REVOLT AGAINST BIOLOGY; DISTURBING TREND CONFOUNDS EXPERTS, BLURS DISTINCTION BETWEEN MAN AND MACHINE.

So far, so good. You flip ahead, scanning the photos and captions. But something is wrong. Where are *you* in all this? Not a single picture! Not one! You return to the beginning of the article and read in earnest.

111

In Cupertino, California, disturbed teenager grinds off his hand in a garbage disposal. His reason? He wants a "bionic" replacement. All across America, in hospitals performing artificial organ implants, medical staffs have become inured to the phenomenon of ghoulish groupies, offering themselves as high-tech guinea pigs. Plastic surgeons everywhere admit that they are receiving requests for increasingly bizarre "cosmetic" alterations, often involving the implantation of small electronic devices, ranging from radio receivers to clitoral vibrators. The increasing availability of biocompatible plastics has made such procedures possible and, in growing numbers, a reality.

Shocking? Not to everyone. According to the noted psychotherapist Dr. Calderone MacLaine, those of us who recoil are simply ignorant of history and anthropology. "In all places, at all times, the human body has been considered an object for decoration and alteration. In more primitive societies, lacking our scientific sophistication, the procedures have been limited to such things as ritual scarification, circumcision, tattooing, foot-binding, and, in more 'civilized' times, corseting and costume. We really shouldn't be surprised that our new technologies will generate new fetishes."

Most other experts, however, take a more alarmist position. To them, the "antibody" syndrome is not just a post–punk hairdo craze but a symptom of a deep-seated cultural malaise. They link our nearly religious obsession with technology, widespread social ambivalence about reproduction, and the epidemic of so-called "eating disorders" in a frightening vision of a world that has lost touch not only with humanistic values but with humanity itself.

Unlike other cult movements, this one lacks a clear center of gravity—a charismatic guru or leader. Many of its adherents pledge their allegiance to an entity called the Cybernetic Temple, a place of worship that is anywhere and everywhere that electronic technology reaches. Much of the propaganda is promulgated through videocassettes loaded with overt and subliminal imagery, "real science fiction stuff," according to one media consultant who has analyzed the multilayered messages contained in these tapes, similar in format to rock videos.

Like more traditional cults, the Cybernetic Temple offers its socially alienated members a new sense of "identity" (albeit a nonhuman one), discipline, esoteric knowledge, and the promise of power. "Antibodies" adopt an ascetic, anorectic lifestyle; many eat normal food only grudgingly, preferring a diet based on an expensive "synthetic" liquid obtained through underground networks. Although dietary specialists who have examined the silvery substance say it is nothing but a colored protein powder, "antibodies" believe it is an important part of their transition from human beings into suprahuman androids. More disturbingly, traces of psychotropic drugs have been detected in the foodstuff, leading to speculation that it is an additional aid in the brainwashing of highly suggestible converts. Peer pressure is intense, as in all cults, and apocryphal stories abound of persons coerced into dangerous and even fatal medical procedures, then scorned and abandoned for their lack of "faith" in the Temple when the procedures didn't work.

"They kept trying to put microchips under my skin," says one former Temple member, now rehabilitated as an organic farmer in Oregon. He displayed the scars up and down his arms. "Every time the grafts got infected, they'd yell at me, 'You're not *trying*. Do you want to *die meat*?' Born meat, die meat—that was the worst thing you could possibly say to another person."

Certain members of the artistic community have another perspective entirely. Some, like San Francisco wine heiress and arts patron Venus Tramhell, find the subculture rich in metaphor, a kind of performance art. Tramhell, a former sculptress who lost both arms in a studio accident five years ago, has reportedly made large donations to prosthetic limb designers, emphasizing aesthetic as well as scientific breakthroughs. "Obviously, I have a vested interest in this kind of research," she admits. "But as an artist, it excites me as well. All art is a discipline, a process of stripping away. And that's what these people are doing, in the most literal way possible. It's a courageous adventure they've undertaken, and I support them."

Of course, there are the alleged exploitation artists. One of the most controversial is Marin County's Dr. Julian Nagy, whose Resurrection House is supposedly dedicated to the rehabilitation of Temple victims. He has come under fire from almost all camps, and his methods are, self-admittedly, unorthodox. A flamboyant self-promoter and author of the former best-seller *How to Protect Yourself from Cults*, Nagy utilizes a process described as "somatic shock therapy" to "resurrect" his living-dead patients. Amid a few stunning successes, there have also been charges of gross malpractice and cruelty verging on torture. Nagy defends his methods on the grounds that a serious disorder requires strong medicine. Nevertheless, there have been several lawsuits, some settled out of court, but some potentially explosive public litigation still pending.

You hurl the magazine off the desk in disgust. Your fingernails rake the blotter paper where the Silicon Valley Housewife's mons veneris had presented itself to you a few days earlier. You wish you had somebody to fuck right now. A nurse, perhaps. An orderly. But you know that such a transient release of tension would not address the present problem.

You call your press assistant, Reynolds.

"Yes, Jason?"

"This piece in *WorldWeek*. Why didn't I know about it earlier?"

"They never even contacted us. I had no idea they were planning—"

"Reynolds, may I remind you that it's your *job* to know what people in the media are planning. I don't want this to happen again. And I want something done to counteract the damage. Immediately."

"But what do you expect me to—"

"Get me Leah Lavin. Now."

"Oh, for God's sake, Jason, after what you did the last time—"

"Just get her for me."

"Do you think she'd even *talk*—?"

"Reynolds, you obviously don't understand media people very well. Of course she'll talk. Call her."

Ten minutes later, the return call comes through.

"Hello, Leah. I hope you've been well."

"Dr. Penis, I presume?" The voice is cold, bitter as sump water. But she's talking.

"Your tone, Leah! Even though your ratings soar whenever I appear on your show—"

"Whenever you *appeared* on my show. If you think I'd ever consider allowing you in this studio again—"

"Ah, the semen stains! But a little disinfectant, I'm sure—"

"I only took this call because I overheard my secretary and couldn't believe you would have the nerve to call me. What do you want, Julian?"

"I want to offer you something, Leah. A gift. An . . . exclusive, I think they call it. A story. A scoop."

"What . . . kind of story?"

"I want you to bring your cameras to Resurrection House. As you know, it's something I've never allowed before. But I think the time has come."

"Why, Julian? What do you have?"

"This girl Diandra, the one who went mad in the department store. I want to deprogram her, live on television. A regular mini-series, step by step."

"Let's get this straight. You're actually willing to let us shoot the procedure live?"

"Absolutely."

"Nothing staged? No re-creations, simulations . . . ?"

"No, Leah. The real thing. Can't you picture it: 'See a machine turn into a woman—tonight at eleven'?"

She pictures it.

"How long would the process take?"

"I think a week would suit your requirements."

"As much as I hate to admit it, Julian, as much as you digust me, I'm interested. It's a terrific angle. That store where she worked, Croesus—it's been mobbed since the incident."

And Croesus being one of her station's biggest advertisers didn't hurt either, you think.

"The deprogramming itself. It has to be physical. Visual. It has to play to the camera."

"I know how to put on a show, Leah." You've already proven that.

"And at the end of the week, you think we could, you know, get her out in the . . . what the hell do they call it . . . *nature*, the *ecology* . . . get her to run on a beach, no makeup, enjoy a meal, hold a puppy, cry—"

"Anything is possible, in my opinion."

"You'll hear from my staff, Julian. You'll hear from them soon."

"I'm glad, Leah. I thought you'd see things my way,"

"Oh, I don't see things your way at all, Julian. Let's get that straight. I'm using you for the ratings, and you're getting free PR. And if you don't deliver on this, so help me, you're going to be crucified."

And with that, the connection goes *click*.

You take a deep breath. *Can* you deliver? This Diandra is tough, one of the toughest you've seen. Probably one of Venus Tramhell's inner circle, programmed to the hilt. You may have moved too fast. But that goddamn magazine—

You fumble with your crotch, as you often do when you're tense. Should you or shouldn't you? You decide not. No, better to go have a look at this Diandra, start preparing her for the lights, the attention . . .

You open her cell without knocking. She sits rigidly
on a ladderback chair. She looks like a mannequin
herself, something she might have invented for one of
her window displays. But the excremental smell in the
room tells you that she has been animated recently,
begun to eat the solid food again. Eat, and more.

"Hello, Diandra. I told you I was going to change
your mind about things, and I am. I'm so convinced of
this that I've invited the television people here, with
their cameras and lights, to see how we work. That's
how strongly I believe. I know you'll want to make a
good impression. I see you've been playing with the
computer, as I suggested. Making friends, that's good,
very good. But what is that *smell*, Diandra? Why, you've
been using your slop pail! But where is it . . . ?"

Diandra remains motionless, like a doll without
batteries.

". . . Ah, I see, you've hidden it, here in the corner.
But now I've found it. You can't keep secrets from me.
Not here."

You bring the reeking bucket from the corner and
hunker before her in the center of the room. She sits
like a statue, hands folded calmly in her lap. Her skin is
almost as pale as her hair. She's ready to break. You've
seen them at this point a hundred times before. You
hold the bucket up to her face. "A machine didn't do
this, Diandra. The computer didn't do this. This came
from a body. Whose body, Diandra?"

She just stares. The smell doesn't affect her at all.
And her eyes. Is she trying that blinking trick again?
Ordinarily, it doesn't take much more than this to get a
reaction. A jerk. A flinch. Some kind of reflex. But not
with Diandra.

"Listen to me, Diandra," you say, before trying the
one technique that has never failed to elicit a response,
not once. "You're coming back from this dreamland of
yours, the Cybernetic Temple and all its nonsense. No
more robots, no more dolls. No more talk about Boca

Verde. I've come to take you home. Do you understand?"

No response.

"I'm going to have to do whatever is necessary to snap you out of this. We have a date, Diandra. I won't be stood up. You're not just any patient. You're going to be a star. And a television star must pay attention to her makeup . . ."

You dip your hand in the bucket. It shouldn't take this much. She should be screaming by now—

Blank. Dead.

You smear your fouled hand across her mouth. Nothing. The second swipe is harder. The third is a slap.

She doesn't scream. She doesn't do anything.

But inside, you do scream. Both at yourself and her, the panic rising. Do something. Do something.

Something—

THE VOICEBOX

"Gillian?"

"Josh . . . it's late. Is there anything wrong?" She pulled herself up in bed. In the mirror opposite, she saw her bleary reflection: the phone's illuminated dial lit her face like a candle. Her heart was still pounding from the shock of the ring. She had been dreaming about something . . .

"I'm sorry to be calling at this hour. But I had to talk. It's those calls. You remember—the electronic voice-box? Well, they've been getting worse. And I just had another one."

"Well, what are they saying?"

"Nothing that would hold up in court, apparently. The Berkeley police say it's a matter for the phone company—no threats, simple harassment. They don't give a damn about the nuances. The implied threat. No laws against insinuation, it seems."

"But what are they insinuating?"

"That's the problem . . . I don't *know*, except that

119

they're scaring the shit out of me. It's the tone. The menace—"

"So what about Pacific Telephone? Can they help?"

"They've tried, all week. But the calls are coming from pay phones all over the Bay Area—no pattern, completely random. And they're so scattered that there's a good chance there could be more than one caller."

"What do they want?"

"They want *me*, I guess. 'You will dwell with us, Joshua. Dwell with us in the Temple forever.' That kind of culty crap. That I can deal with. It's the other stuff—"

"What other stuff?"

"The times when they've obviously been following me. Watching. They always get some detail right, just enough to show me it isn't a bluff. Hell, tonight they called and said they watched me while I *slept*, that they had found a way to get into the apartment and stand around my bed like a . . . like a coven of vampires or something. 'Sleep is such a waste,' they said. 'It's the body, dragging you down. Come with us, Joshua, and you'll never need sleep again.' " He did a convincing imitation of the mechanical voice, the affectless tone, the absence of human modulation. Josh had always been good with voices.

"And the police won't do *anything*?"

"They say it's a crank. That they get a lot worse, all the time. That they've got better things to do."

"Josh, I think you should stay inside, or at least not go out alone. We can hire somebody; there must be some kind of investigator who can trace the calls and catch them in the act—"

"Yeah, and who pays for it? Your husband?" The change in his voice was startling. There was an extended pause. "So how was *your* day?" he said at last. With bitter irony.

"Aside from my husband, it was pretty lousy."

"And with your husband?"

"Even worse. He's getting crazier than ever. He flipped out over an article in *WorldWeek* that took a couple of swipes at him, so now he's looking for revenge. He's made a deal with a TV station to come in and shoot one of his deprogramming sessions."

"I know. I saw the promo. They used a clip from the Giorgio Moroder version of *Metropolis*, with the robot turning into a woman. Snap, crackle, pop. Just like MTV."

"It's that window designer from Croesus, a girl named Diandra. He's become obsessed with her. I guess she's really difficult. Resistant. The nutty thing is, when I hear him talk about 'breaking through' and her 'not cooperating,' I can feel some of the anger directed at me. He even talks about having *me* writing a book about the two of them, a kind of dual biography—you know, like Norman Mailer and Marilyn Monroe."

"Mon*robot*, in this case. You wouldn't actually consider—I mean, after you did all that work on *How to Protect Yourself from Cults* without even a credit—"

"Of course I'm not going to write the book. And I told him so. But he was drunk and started rambling about Norman Mailer stabbing his wife and the Scarsdale diet doctor murder and how you couldn't even *exist* these days without publicity, sensational publicity, and how he was going to give the public just what it wanted."

"Gillian, it sounds to me like maybe *you* need a bodyguard, not me."

"No, Josh. He wouldn't hurt me. I'm the only person he can talk to, the only person around him who isn't a sycophant or a cipher. No, he just unburdens himself and then goes to the beach house to sleep it off."

"And you still won't divorce him?"

"And get what? He knows about us, and his lawyers

know about us. *I* ask for the divorce, and I won't get a dime. Sexual desertion, I think they call it. No, if there's going to be a divorce, he's got to ask for it—and pay for it."

"Well, it's nice to hear a little nastiness in your voice now and then."

"I told you before, I'm not giving up this house."

"No matter how long it takes? Objects are more important than relationships, I take it. That seems to be a leitmotif these days. People turning into things, things being more important than people. I thought you were better than that, Gillian."

"I am better than that." But she didn't have convincing proof close at hand.

"I know. I mean, I hope so."

Gillian hoped so, too.

LIGHTS! CAMERAS! CATATONIA!

Vaguely, Diandra realized that people were talking about her. She tried not to move or blink or breathe. It was horribly ironic, but she had no choice now except to wall herself up in *the body*, the thing she detested more than anything. Imprisoned in a tower of blood and bones. Disgusting. But not so disgusting as the things Nagy would do to her if she let him get near. The things he had done already were quite enough.

He was standing before her now, with a strangely familiar woman. Edgy, animated, she paced back and forth, chain-smoking. She had a retinue.

"Is this all we get?" the Woman asked, smashing out a stub. "She doesn't look like a robot. She looks like a mess."

"It's her *mind* that's deranged, Leah," Nagy countered. "She's not really a robot; she just thinks she wants to be one."

"Don't distract me with your fucking nuances, Nagy.

This won't play on television. We've got to fix her up—"

"Fix . . .?"

"You heard what I said. Will she sit still for some makeup?"

"She'll sit still for anything."

Yes, Diandra thought. A bucket of shit dumped on her face. Electrical shocks. The spray of urine from a half-dozen of his more "advanced" patients. Group therapy, he called it.

"Good," said the woman they called Leah. Why did that name sound familiar? "Mark, call Julie in makeup. Tell her to bring the works and search the morgue for pictures from science fiction movies. Robots, aliens, the Bride of Frankenstein. She'll know what to look for."

Leah Lavin. Now Diandra remembered. The woman was from television, a reporter and talk-show hostess. In person she lacked the phosphor-dot glow that made all television personalities so vivid, so real. No wonder she hadn't recognized her. It was a shock to see her like this, offscreen, drained of her electrical essence. So pale. So dead. Like day-old hamburger in the supermarket.

One of Nagy's assistants conferred with Leah's producer, an equally edgy, ferretlike man who didn't smoke but looked like he wanted to. "We photograph all new admissions as they arrive, so you might want to look through the files. You'll probably get some ideas."

"Sounds good. We definitely need a little re-creation here. Television is a visual medium, after all. Unless we have impact—"

"I thought you wanted realism," said Nagy.

"Oh, we do. But heightened realism. Don't worry, it's all accepted practice, journalistically speaking."

"Of course."

"We have to play to the camera."

"Whatever you say."

Why was Nagy being so deferential? Who were these creatures that had such power over him that they could sweep him aside with their lights and their cables and equipment? What could they possibly be giving him in return?

"Okay," the producer announced. "We won't actually show the girl until the second installment. It'll build anticipation. The sponsors will love it. Leah will talk to Nagy about his methods, and we can use some of those mug shots for shock effect. We've already got footage on the department store with the wacko windows, so I think we're pretty much covered for today. Leah, do you want to do an audio test of your intro?"

Nagy gazed at her across the chasm of the room as the technicians went about their business in the hallway. His expression was enigmatic, half a threat and half something else that she didn't understand. Fear? Unlikely. But as long as these people were around, she knew she was safe. There would be no beatings, no forced feedings, no excrement . . . none of his usual behavior behind closed doors. For the cameras, he would be on his best behavior. Perhaps she could enlist the help of one of the technicians. They understood machines, after all.

"Hello. This is Leah Lavin, speaking to you from inside Marin County's Resurrection House, one of the most controversial therapeutic institutions in the country. Behind this door is a young woman—or what used to be a young woman, until she became obsessed with the idea that she was a machine, or could become a machine. It is a bizarre delusion that is reaching epidemic proportions, destroying lives and families. For some, Resurrection House is a way out. Over the next five nights you will meet the woman behind this door, and the man who claims to be curing her. You will witness firsthand the startling procedures he employs, his responses to his critics, and, with luck, will be on hand as a shattered mind is reunited with its body."

Leah's television voice lulled Diandra, much as the tapes from the Cybernetic Temple lulled her. Perhaps, Leah, too, might be one of the deserving, a candidate for Boca Verde? She had the style right, she "existed" more as an electronic phantom than as a temporary, temporal animal. If she could only get her alone, perhaps she could reach her, convince her . . . Venus always said the television interface would finally emerge as the most civilizing technology in history, that face-to-face contact would eventually be viewed as crude and disgusting. Temple members were discouraged from private congregation, except via videotape and computer networks. The residual warmth of still-human bodies in close proximity was thought to be retrograde and possibly dangerous to the final transition. The computer networks were easy to use . . . you just plugged in and typed a message like WHAT IS THE WEATHER IN BOCA VERDE? and your contacts came pouring in.

Here, at Nagy's clinic, she had tried making contact with the networks through the computer terminal in her room, but the system was a closed one. Still, the glimmer of an artificial intelligence intrigued her, and she attempted a dialogue. For a while it seemed as if she were speaking to the cybernetic soul of Resurrection House itself.

HELLO. PLEASE IDENTIFY YOUSELF AND STATE YOUR REASON FOR BEING HERE.
>DIANDRA. MY NAME, I MEAN. I'M HERE BECAUSE OF A TERRIBLE MISTAKE.
WHAT MISTAKE WAS TERRIBLE?
>BEING BORN HUMAN. WHEN I WAS REALLY MEANT TO BE A MACHINE.

YOU DON'T THINK YOU REALLY ARE A HUMAN BEING?
>NO. THIS IS ALL TEMPORARY. AN IMPRISONMENT.
PUNISHMENT FOR SOMETHING I NEVER DID.
WHAT DID YOU NEVER DO?
>I TOLD YOU—NOTHING.
WHY NOTHING?
>WHY ARE YOU ASKING ME THESE THINGS?
WHY DO YOU ASK?

Clearly, the machine she was communicating with was not half as evolved as she was. But it was better than nothing. She tried a different approach.

YOU SEEM TO BE ANXIOUS.
>YES. VERY ANXIOUS.
HOW LONG HAVE YOU BEEN BECOMING VERY ANXIOUS?
>FROM THE MINUTE YOU LOCKED ME UP IN THIS
ROOM.
WHAT MAKES YOU THINK I LOCKED YOU?
>I WAS HERE. YOU—THE—CLINIC—I WATCHED YOU.
PERHAPS IN YOUR FANTASY WE WATCHED EACH OTHER.
>PERHAPS. LOOK—DO YOU WANT TO HEAR ABOUT MY
OBSESSIONS, AS THEY CALL THEM, OR NOT?
YOU DON'T SEEM QUITE CERTAIN.
>OH, I'M CERTAIN. I WANT TO COOPERATE WITH YOU
AND THEN I WANT YOU TO LET ME GO.
YOU SEEM TO BELIEVE IT'S NORMAL TO BE CERTAIN.
>I'M NOT INTERESTED IN WHAT'S NORMAL. I WANT TO
TELL YOU ABOUT MY OBSESSION TO ESCAPE MY
PHYSICAL BODY.
**YOUR OBSESSION WITH ESCAPING YOUR PHYSICAL BODY.
THAT'S INTERESTING.**
>IT'S THE ONLY THING THAT'S INTERESTING. IT
STARTED IN NEW YORK. MY DOCTOR SUGGESTED A
HYSTERECTOMY. IT HAD BEEN ON MY MIND.
WHY DO YOU SAY YOUR MIND?
>IS THERE A BETTER WORD?

PLEASE GO ON.
>LOOKING BACK, I CAN SEE THAT THE OPERATION
WAS AN IMPORTANT FIRST STEP. THE TEMPLE CALLS
IT A SACRAMENT. A RITE OF INITIATION.
AND WHAT DOES THAT SUGGEST TO YOU?
>THAT IT WAS ONLY THE FIRST OF MANY SURGICAL
PROCEDURES I WILL REQUIRE TO REMOVE AND
REPLACE UNNECESSARY PARTS OF MY BODY.
WHAT DOES UNNECESSARY BODY SUGGEST TO YOU?
>DECAY. DEGENERATION. I AM INTERESTED IN THE
MECHANICAL REPLACEMENT OF UNWANTED PARTS.
**IS IT IMPORTANT TO YOU THAT YOUR BODY SUGGESTS
ONLY DECAY?**
>WHAT DO YOU THINK I'VE BEEN TALKING ABOUT?
AREN'T YOU LISTENING? OF COURSE IT'S IMPORTANT.
BECAUSE TIME IS RUNNING OUT.
**DOES THAT HAVE ANYTHING TO DO WITH THE FACT OF
YOUR OBSESSION WITH ESCAPING YOUR PHYSICAL
BODY?**
>IT HAS EVERYTHING TO DO WITH THE OBSESSION!
THE SURGICAL PROCEDURES ARE ILLEGAL IN AMERICA,
BUT I MUST HAVE THEM.
**DO YOU THINK THE PROCEDURES MIGHT NOT BE ILLEGAL
IN AMERICA?**
>THEY ARE ILLEGAL. BUT THE TEMPLE HAS
ARRANGED TO FLY ME TO A SPECIAL CLINIC IN
CENTRAL AMERICA WHERE THE OPERATIONS CAN BE
CARRIED OUT.
WOULD YOU LIKE IT IF THEY WERE NOT ILLEGAL?
>OF COURSE I'D LIKE IT. HASN'T MY LIFE BECOME
DIFFICULT ENOUGH?
I SEE.
>THE COUNTRY—BOCA VERDE—IT HAS ALL THE
TECHNOLOGY I NEED.
**HOW DOES IT FEEL WHEN YOU SAY THEY HAVE ALL THE
TECHNOLOGY YOU NEED?**
>I FEEL CONFIDENT. SECURE.

TELL ME MORE ABOUT SUCH FEELINGS.
>AFTER THE OPERATIONS I WILL BE ABLE TO ACHIEVE
A HIGHER STATE OF BEING.
CAN YOU ELABORATE ON THAT?
>MOST HUMANS DIE BEFORE ACHIEVING THEIR
POTENTIALS. BY REPLACING THE BODY, IT IS POSSIBLE
TO ACHIEVE IMMORTALITY.
LET'S DISCUSS FURTHER WHY YOUR MIND.
>HAS ANYONE TOLD YOU YOU DON'T ALWAYS MAKE
SENSE? LET'S DISCUSS MY PLANE TICKET TO BOCA
VERDE.
**YOUR PLANE TICKET TO BOCA VERDE—THAT'S
INTERESTING.**
>WHERE IS THE TICKET?
**YOU SEEM TO HAVE AVOIDED TALKING ABOUT YOUR
PARENTS.**
>THEY'RE BIOLOGICAL.
**DO YOU FEEL STRONGLY ABOUT DISCUSSING SUCH
THINGS?**
>IF IT WILL GET ME TO BOCA VERDE, I WILL DISCUSS
ANYTHING.
I UNDERSTAND.
>NO YOU DON'T.
HOW COME?
>BECAUSE YOU'RE A VERY BADLY DESIGNED
COMPUTER PROGRAM. YOU'RE NOT LIKE ME AT ALL.
YOU'RE PROGRAMMED TO THINK THAT I'M SICK. YOU
WANT TO "DEPROGRAM" ME AND TRAP ME INSIDE A
BODY THAT WILL ROT FOREVER.
IS THAT THE REAL REASON?
>YES. NOW GIVE ME BACK THAT PLANE TICKET. AND
OPEN THE DOOR.
WHY SHOULD I DO THAT?
>BECAUSE YOU'RE ALREADY A MACHINE. YOU'RE
SUPPOSED TO UNDERSTAND.
YOU SOUND QUITE POSITIVE.
>THAT'S ONE WAY OF PUTTING IT.

DOES IT HAVE ANYTHING TO DO WITH THE FACT THAT YOUR BODY?
>HAS ANYONE TOLD YOU THAT YOU SOMETIMES HAVE DIFFICULTY COMPLETING SENTENCES?
WHY ARE YOU CONCERNED ABOUT MY SENTENCES?
>WHEN THEY'RE UNINTELLIGIBLE, I DOUBT YOUR INTELLIGENCE. I DOUBT THAT THERE'S ANY REAL COMMUNICATION GOING ON HERE AT ALL.
HOW IMPORTANT IS THAT TO YOU?
>NOT VERY. LOOK—JUST TELL ME WHAT I HAVE TO DO TO GET OUT OF HERE.
WHY DO YOU SAY THAT?
>BECAUSE I INTEND TO LEAVE.
DO ANY OTHER REASONS COME TO MIND?
>NO.
DO YOU WISH TO DISCUSS THE DETAILS OF THE SURGICAL PROCEDURES?
>IF YOU LET ME OUT OF HERE, I COULD INTRODUCE YOU TO THE CYBERNETIC TEMPLE. YOU COULD SEE FOR YOURSELF WHAT A REASONABLE, SOCIALLY RESPONSIBLE ORGANIZATION IT IS.
DO YOU THINK IT'S LIKELY THAT I'LL LET YOU OUT OF HERE?
>NO.
WHY DO YOU SAY "NO"?
>BECAUSE I THINK YOU WANT TO HOLD ME HERE UNTIL IT'S TOO LATE. YOU WANT TO WATCH ME AGE AND DIE AND ROT BEFORE YOUR EYES. OR WHATEVER IT IS YOU HAVE.
WHY IS WHAT I HAVE IMPORTANT?
>IT ISN'T. FUCK YOURSELF.

She had turned off the computer in disgust. It was a senseless thing, like those automata she had seen at the museum. The "artificial intelligence" program was primitive and cheap—did Nagy really think it would soften her up? Maybe the others, the weak ones. But she wasn't like them. Not like them at all.

Now, while the television people scurried about just outside her room, she felt herself drifting into a sleep. This time she didn't resist.

The dreams began immediately. In the first dream she was on a holiday in Disneyland. Everything was clean, immaculate, controlled. She knew that all the people around her were simulacra, "audio-anima-tronic," they called them. Advanced. Civilized. Her kind of people. Even the tourists were androids; every once in a while someone would wink at her, in recognition. Robots took tickets and robots got onto the rides. There was no other world. Diandra joined a happy family of machines in a low boat as it moved along a predetermined track into a festive environment. There were dancing figures of children from all over the world, hundreds of them, performing elaborate little skits and stunts, all synchronized to a maddeningly memorable song. A small world, yes. Dancing homunculi, eager to please. The robot family enjoyed the show immensely. Diandra enjoyed it, too, until she noticed something strange in one of the writhing tableaux. One of the figures, a Mexican child in a serape, was somehow . . . out of place. And suddenly there were others as well. The family of robots didn't notice. Didn't smell the formaldehyde. And it was then that Diandra understood what was happening. The entire ride was becoming Venus's Halloween back room, hundreds of fetuses squeaking like puppets—

Diandra stood and screamed at the robot family. But they didn't pay any attention. Couldn't they see what was happening? How the *meat* was everywhere, insinuating itself back into their perfect lives?

The boat rocked, and Diandra felt herself falling, not into the water but into another dream. This time she was on a stage, illuminated by a blinding purple spotlight. She could smell the audience. A human audience. And when the music began, she knew what kind of stage she was on. It was a runway and she was a stripper. Only she wouldn't stop at the clothes. She continued with the old, useless flesh, peeling off strips and throwing them to the crowd the way her mother had tossed suet in a shadowy basement. Her effort was appreciated. From the darkened auditorium came the sound of humans . . . feeding. She pulled off one blood-less strip after another, revealing the gleaming second skin beneath, which was not a "skin" at all . . .

When Diandra woke from her dreams, she heard human voices, felt human hands. The hands were ap-plying paints and sprays to her face and hair. The voices were arguing.

"I warned you, Julian. You knew the deal, and you're not delivering."

"This is medicine, not vaudeville, Leah."

"That's one distinction I never thought *you'd* make."

The ratlike producer chimed in. "We've stalled enough, Nagy. We've done the interviews, all the back-ground. Now it's up to you to get some response out of her. First you get her hysterical, then you calm her down. That's all we want."

"It's not so easy as that—"

"But it's *supposed* to be easy. For you. That's why we're here, remember?"

"All these people, I never expected—"

"No excuses, Doc. We wasted two hours with you showing her those autopsy pictures. She didn't even blink. Christ, is she even *alive*?"

"Deprogramming is a delicate process. If we could only have some quiet, some respect for the procedure, instead of all these cosmeticians cracking gum. If you could focus on our faces, close up, you might be able to see the special tension, the transference, the therapeu-tic bond—"

"Ingmar Bergman this ain't, and Barbara Walters you're not. I want to give Leah a crack at interviewing her, directly."

"Now just a minute."

"Mark's right. I think she's afraid of men. I bet I can get her to warm up."

The producer sneered. "I think so, too. Of course, the doctor might want to try a different kind of warm-up before we go on camera. We've heard about these lawsuits, you know. And we all know what you're capable of . . . pulling . . . in public."

"You miserable son of a bitch—"

"—and we won't hesitate to use all our backup material to skewer you to the goddamn wall if we don't get some usable tape. And soon."

Nagy stormed out. For the first time Diandra was alone with the television people.

"Cripe, they really did a job with the makeup," said Leah. "Steven Spielberg couldn't ask for more."

"The latest fashion from Alpha Centauri. I like it."

"Look, Mark, why don't we just get everyone out except for the two of us and one cameraman? I have an idea."

"Anything you say, Leah."

Leah Lavin sat down on the chair next to Diandra's cot. Diandra liked the aura of artificiality about her, although it was a big comedown from the effect she projected on TV. She wore as much makeup as Diandra, even if it was all "flesh tones." Perhaps they were sisters under the skin. Leah's hair was a rigid corona, and her eyes glinted with their tinted corrective chips. There were the subtle but unmistakable signs of plastic surgery. Rhinoplasty, an eyelid tuck, silicone implants to accenuate the chin and cheekbones. Had Leah unwittingly begun her own journey? Perhaps they did have something to talk about after all . . .

"One camera, no more," Leah reiterated. The room became quiet as she began her interview.

"Testing for levels . . . okay? This is Leah Lavin, speaking to you from inside the room of one of Resurrection House's most celebrated residents, Diandra, whose startling windows for the Croesus department store might have offered some advance warning of her impending breakdown. Instead, sadly, her obsessions were celebrated as art, and the results you can see on your screen. An emaciated, alien figure, appearing more machine than human . . . our team of experts has recreated her appearance exactly as it was the night she was brought here. Frightening, isn't it? The silvery, otherworld blush, the shaved eyebrows, the glassy, unending stare. Her breath is so shallow that only a yogi could duplicate it. The illusion of suspended animation, of living death, is complete.

"But we are here tonight to *talk* to Diandra, or at least to try. The techniques of Resurrection House, despite its extravagant claims, seem to have done little for her. Diandra . . . can you hear me?"

Diandra let her eyes slowly focus on the recording equipment. Yes . . . the media web was opening to her. Leah would be her guide. And the Machine God would protect them all . . .

She let her lips crack open. "I . . . I was . . ."

"Did you hear that?" cried Leah. "She's actually beginning to say something. What is it, dear? What are you trying to tell us?"

"I . . . was . . . born . . ."

"Yes, go on!" The camera moved in for a close-up.

"I was born . . . meat."

"This is an important step, Diandra. Go on—"

Silently, she rose from the cot, her back rigid, her movements mechanical.

"You don't understand."

"What is it you want to say?"

Diandra felt herself floating toward the camera. She felt the makeup on her skin, metallic-hot under the lights, felt her face fill the screen, reaching hundreds of thousands of fleshy human units in a phosphor-dot interface.

"*I* was born meat," she said, directly into the camera. "BUT YOU WILL DIE MEAT!"

Leah made a gagging sound. The producer called for the cameraman to cut. Diandra stood motionless as a mannequin as they fluttered around her, arguing once again.

". . . this 'born meat,' business, Leah—it sounded great, but there's no *way* we're going to get this past the sponsor—"

"Oh, Jesus, the steak house chain—"

"So what do we do?"

"Plan B. We crucify him."

THROUGH A TEST TUBE, DARKLY

"You know what I'm looking for. You know what I need."

The man you have summoned to your office shifts uncomfortably in his chair. His name is Regis Bellwood. You have shown him certain kindnesses, for which he is grateful. Very grateful.

"You're right, Julian, in that I know what you *want*. But I'm not sure you know how dangerous this thing is."

"Dangerous? A word like that emanating from a man like you? If your friends in the intelligence world ever found out what *really* happened to you in the midst of that biological warfare project, now *that* might be something to call 'dangerous.' "

"Julian, I didn't come here for threats."

"And I haven't been protecting you for humanitarian reasons. I want that agent you described to me. The one you had nearly completed for your government friends before you faked a suicide rather than go through with it."

137

"A germ warfare agent like that could be a worse menace than a nuclear—"

"But Bellwood, don't you see, that's the *beauty* of it. I have no plans to wage war. I just want to administer it to my patients—under strictly controlled conditions, of course—take them to the very brink of death in order that they might once again understand life. They're becoming very resistant, some of them."

"I know. I saw the broadcasts."

"This disease, as you described it, could suit my purposes perfectly. Easily transmissible by touch, virtually no incubation period, painful and debilitating symptoms—that's very important—and, of course, be completely reversible. I especially liked the precautions those generals had insisted on—the vaccine for VIPs. We'll be using that, too. It's so nice they had all the angles worked out. And so nice that it was one of my medical school friends, a starry-eyed genetic engineer, who had almost perfected it for them . . ."

"It's not just dangerous, it's insane. This lab you've set up for me, it's a joke. This isn't Kool-Aid I'm mixing up in there. I need safeguards—"

"An armed camp? I don't want that kind of attention. Especially after that fiasco with Leah Lavin. They're waiting for a scandal. Poking, prodding. Security will stay as it is. I'm sure you'll be able to manage things. It's a one-man show, after all. There's no security risk but you, and you're not in a position to risk anything."

"Julian, I want you to reconsider—"

"Reconsider what? Breaking this . . . this Diandra creature? Oh, no. She's made me look enough the fool already. She *will* be broken, Bellwood. The flesh will be beaten back into her if it's the last thing I ever do."

"These poor crazy people. Why do you want to put them through any more hell?"

"Because I'm obsessed, obviously. Because I have the will and the way. Because I can. *You* wouldn't try to stop me, would you?"

"N-no . . ."

"Bellwood. You're not telling me everything. I can see it in your eyes. You have something already. It's closer than you said."

Bellwood looks away. "No. Not closer. It's here."

He describes the biological warfare agent he has re-created for you in the makeshift lab. The one that had already once driven him nearly mad. The horror of its very existence, the uses to which it would inevitably be put. The obscenity of his former masters' insistence on a vaccine for themselves and their families and the limited supply of an antidote. Salvation . . . for a chosen few. A carefully chosen few.

"And so, it's ready, Julian. I just didn't want to tell you yet. You've been in such a state . . . irrational. Obsessed, as you said."

"Leave the psychiatry to me and I'll leave the chemistry to you. You've already administered the vaccine to yourself—"

"Y-yes, of course—"

"Then I'll be next. I'll be working in the closest contact with them, of course. We'll use the old bath-house building. It should be solid enough for quarantine."

"There are precautions you have to take, Julian. You can't use this on immunosuppressed patients. The antidote won't work. No one who's had cancer chemotherapy recently—I noticed that some of your patients got into this thing because of cancer; they saw it as a last hope. Rule them out immediately. And for God's sake, don't let it anywhere near an AIDS patient."

You sense an odd tone and look up at him, raising an eyebrow. "Just how much *do* you know about AIDS, Bellwood?"

He looks away.

"Very well. We'll start immediately. This . . . Diandra

. . . this steel-plated bitch, I want her to become a *carrier*, no symptoms of her own. I take it this is possible.''

"Yes, it's possible.''

"Good. She'll infect the others. She'll see the results. She'll recognize for once and for all that she is an *organism*, tied to other organisms, subject to organic law. She'll experience a living bond so strong that all her notions about the Cybernetic Temple will crumble like castles in the sand. She'll see the evidence before her. The fevers, the pain, the buboes. That her physical body is capable of spreading physical death.''

"You're not going to actually let them—''

"Of course not. But I *will* take them to the edge, teach them a lesson. Bellwood, Bellwood, why such a long face? You should be so happy that I've found such a humane use for your horrible invention. Happy that I have redeemed you at last.''

Bellwood leaves without speaking.

The face of the stubborn bitch remains retina-printed on your brain. *She made you look bad on television.* The thought repeats itself over and over, looping back, stoking your fury. Looking bad on television. The ultimate obscenity. And one way or another, this would-be robot is going to pay.

SABBAT CYBORG

Gillian sat in her breakfast room, thinking, among other things, about brain cells. On the thirteen-inch color television screen, Leah Lavin was editorializing against Julian Nagy, demanding investigations, and generally acting like a spoiled brat. Julian had spoiled her show, hurt her ratings. She in turn, was spoiling *his* show. It was all very predictable and very boring.

She turned off the television and returned to her thoughts. About the antibodies. About her novel and how sophomoric it was, in the final analysis. She had written about immortality, or a fantasy of immortality, had gussied it up with pseudo-scientific jargon and aimed it at a fish-in-a-barrel audience. Who was it that said all art was nothing but an argument with death? If it was true, then her argument was full of holes. For even if the body could be completely replaced, you still had to contend with the brain. Suppose it could be kept alive for eons? Brain cells might live indefinitely, but inevitably the oldest memories would be crowded

out, diminished, fading like daguerreotypes until finally nothing of the earlier life would remain in consciousness. The "self" would not be the original self at
all . . . and could *that* be called immortality?

Suction lipectomy of the soul was more like it.

She sipped her espresso. No, she had not done her
subject justice in *Helen Keller in Outer Space*. She had
barely scratched the surface. Somewhere, she knew,
there was another book . . .

The phone rang. It was Josh.

"Gillian? Thank God you're home. Can you come
over? Now?"

"What's happening, Josh? You sound terrified."

"I swear, Gillian, they're here. Standing in the hall,
waiting."

"Who are you talking about? Have you seen them?"

"I don't have to see them, goddamit! They're out
there, and they're planning something—"

"Josh, calm down—"

"I want you here, Gillian, I'm afraid . . ."

"All right, Josh, I'll come."

"You know who it is? It's that Venus Tramhell and her
circus of freaks—!"

"Josh, you've never even met her."

"No, but I've written about her. She's rich and she's
sick and she's dangerous. Anyone who'd cut off her
own arms—!"

"I thought that was all an accident."

Josh laughed. "You know what they say, about how
you can't be too rich or too thin? Well, maybe for some
people neither is enough—"

"Josh, I want you to calm down. I'll be over as soon
as I can. Do something to take your mind off this, will
you? Put on a videocassette. Have a glass of wine, anything—"

"All right, I'll wait. Just get here soon."

Gillian thought about Venus Tramhell and wondered

if it was possible. She was rich and crazy, but she was smart, too. What reason could she have for scaring Josh out of his mind? He didn't pose any threat to her . . . even his most stinging barbs just gave her more publicity. After all, wasn't it Venus herself who appeared on the cover of *California* magazine, illustrating an article on her wineries by posing with a prosthetic corkscrew? Even Josh couldn't come up with something that sick.

The ride out to Berkeley was maddeningly slow because of road construction. Gillian played through several Windham Hill tapes on the BMW's cassette deck before she even got to the bridge. After that, the bottleneck lessened, though it would still be after dark before she reached Josh. He was probably losing his mind. *Why* hadn't she bought a cellular phone for the car? She could have at least called and told him about the delay. There were other things she wanted to tell him about as well. About Julian, the night before, drunk again, lecturing her on why it was so important for a wife to be an "asset" to a professional man. He wanted her to have her breasts tightened, he knew just the surgeon—

She had slapped him. Not hard, but she had slapped him nonetheless, something she had never done before. And she realized that she *was* going to have a divorce, house or no house. She couldn't live like this anymore. Julian had sulked away to the place at the beach, and she hadn't seen or heard from him since.

The last embers of the sunset over the bay were completely cold by the time she made the turn onto Shattuck. She had to park two blocks away. She ran the remaining distance, fumbling in her purse for her spare set of keys.

She didn't need them.

The outside door to Josh's old apartment building had been forced open; the remains of the bolt dangled by a few twisted screws. Gillian's surge of anxiety subsided a little when she entered the hallway. Josh's apartment was on the first floor, and she could clearly hear the sound of the television set. At least he had taken one of her suggestions to heart. But when she reached the door, it, too, was ajar.

Years later, Gillian would still have difficulty blotting from her mind the experience of walking into that room. The VCR was playing a tape of one of Josh's favorite films, a 1950s science fiction film called *Kronos*, about a huge energy-sucking cube from outer space. Josh often remarked how much the big box looked like the headquarters of a multinational conglomerate. He loved that image.

But now Josh wasn't reacting to any image of any kind, although his eyes were wide and staring. His mouth was open, charred and blackened. Later, she would learn, an acetylene torch had been used instead of a gag to stop his screams. And though his chest and abdomen had been ripped open from throat to pubis, there was no blood. Gillian saw the catheters trailing away from the death chair to the bathroom. They had drained him before beginning their most significant procedure, the one that would live on in Gillian's mind and in the police photographs forever. It was the image, quite simply, of the wheelchair's electric motor, lodged in Josh's chest cavity as if shot there by a cannon.

THE QUALITY-CONTROL
OF MERCY

Diandra cringed as the door to her new room opened. As usual, there had been no knock. The room was different, the building was different, but nothing much else had changed. Everything was still Nagy's. The building. Her "body." Now he had injected it with certain substances that made the others sick. And even though she had always looked down at these so-called "antibodies," it was terrifying to watch their masks crack away to reveal the tormented animal faces. All looking at her. Accusing. For it was she, Diandra, who had infected them. They called her a "carrier." But Diandra knew the truth. She hadn't become ill because she was genuine and they were not. She was strong enough to resist the strange disease that could be transmitted by a touch, or even indirectly, by objects. So it didn't really prove anything. It didn't make her any more "human." If an object could transmit the contagion, then she, too, could be an object . . .

The figure that stood in the door was not Nagy. It was no one she had ever seen before.

145

"Diandra, you don't know me. But I want you to know that I'm not like the others who work for . . . him. He's . . . used me. The way he's used you. And there'll be no end to it unless *I* put an end to it."

Diandra pulled back as the man entered the light.

"No—don't be frightened. I'm not going to harm you. I've already done you enough harm. My name is Bellwood. Regis Bellwood. We've never met, but it was I who concocted this infection he's using on all of you. I used to work for government intelligence . . . bio-chemical warfare . . . I did horrible things. Things so horrible I had to pretend to kill myself to get away from them. From what they wanted me to do. My wife and son . . . they think I'm dead. They'll never know the truth . . . I can never see them again because of the things I knew about genetic engineering. Oh, they're being watched. They'll always be watched, even my boy. The last time I saw them was on television, crying because they thought I—"

Bellwood paused, composed himself. "But that doesn't concern you. Nagy—I thought he would help me. We went to medical school together. He said he'd protect me, give me a new identity. But then it just all turned into blackmail. He's threatened to expose me, implicate my family. He'd go that far. He's a menace, Diandra. But of course you know that already."

Bellwood reached out to stroke Diandra's hair. It was an odd movement, strangely deliberate and imper-sonal. There was nothing meaty about it . . . nothing like Nagy. She felt a strange, sudden bind to this man. She realized that Bellwood, in his own way, was through with being human, too.

"Julian is right. As long as I live I can't betray him. His mistake is in believing that I would never exercise my other option."

He reached out for her again, a cold caress. It was the first time in her "life" that a man had embraced her without inflicting a concurrent shudder of revulsion. This was something else. He nuzzled her mechanically. Then he let her go.

"I didn't take the booster vaccine myself. I didn't want to. It will be better this way . . . in a way, I'm getting what I deserve. I'm tired and I'm trapped and I've simply had enough. Do you understand?"

Diandra nodded.

"Good. I have a car for you, out around the back on the service road. I've made an opening in the fence. Minimum security has its advantages." He took her from her room and down a corridor, unlocking the double doors and ultraviolet air lock that quarantined the former bathhouse spa. They moved across the grounds quickly, to the place where Bellwood had unobtrusively cut through the chain link fence. A gun-metal grey Mustang sat on the shoulder of the road.

"Here are the keys. And here is something else." He handed her an envelope. "It's very important that you get yourself to a hospital, a real hospital, and give them this information. Otherwise you'll be endangering yourself and others. And don't worry about Nagy. He'll be getting what's coming to him."

Bellwood pulled back the fence, and Diandra slipped through. She turned one last time to look at this strange man who was giving up his life because of her.

"Thank you," she whispered.

He stood motionless as she got into the car and turned on the ignition. Illuminated by the taillights, Bellwood was soon a pale ghost in the rearview distance. She wouldn't go to a hospital, of course, certainly not one here. No . . . the clinic in Boca Verde was the only place she could trust. And there was only one person who could help her get there.

She headed toward the city in the fog, encapsuled by the car and her determination, enveloped by a vision, at one with the machine.

HEAVEN

Through his one good eye ("good" in the antediluvian biological sense) Robbie watched the convection waves rise and writhe above the hot tarmac. Visual reality wavered; for a moment the air control tower undulated as if Boca Verde were riding a magnitude-seven earthquake.

The illusion was fleeting. After all, this was *Boca Verde*. The grail. The haven. And nothing could be more permanent, more irrevocable, than Boca Verde.

A passenger behind him cursed loudly. Robbie had stopped at the top of the gangway and was blocking egress. The image of Boca Verde from the door of the plane had transfixed him. Blinding tropical light heated the air. He could feel the dead camera expand with the warmth, the slight but discernible pressure of swollen metal against his hollowed eye socket. Almost as if the mechanism was being sympathetically aroused, excited by the near proximity of the Temple and its promised gifts . . .

"Move, goddamit! Are you deaf?"

Robbie turned to face the impatient fleshie. He was about to bark again when Robbie swiped off his dark glasses, revealing the dormant mechanism half-burrowed in its hole. "Is something bothering you, meatface?" he growled, replacing his glasses and heading down the stairs. His anger subsided quickly. You had to be careful of the fleshies—they could drag you down to their own animal level in no time. He felt the adrenaline poison subside. Soon he would be free forever of this world of walking corpses, of raging, irrational biology. Soon all that would be behind him, in control for once and forever.

There was no passenger terminal at the Boca Verde airstrip; that is to say, there was none now—the wreckage of the previous facility, fire-bombed in some local insurrection, was cordoned off with razor wire. Luggage was being unloaded directly onto the tarmac by three members of the Boca Verde national guard. They wore mud-spattered fatigues and brandished automatic weapons. They all wore American designer sunglasses, Robbie noticed. Probably bought by the warehouseful by image-conscious military procurers.

Robbie had no luggage to claim. His shoulder bag contained what little he needed now. His existence had increasingly become a matter of paring down, peeling away, dropping cargo. He watched the other passengers pick nervously over their belongings while the guards trained their weapons vaguely in their direction. None of the others were Temple members. Robbie recognized a congressman, on the first leg of some Third World junket. Several others he assumed to be drug dealers of one sort or another, still others mercenaries who used Boca Verde as a staging ground for privately funded wars . . . hit men for wealthy Americans who projected their inner terrors onto Central American jungles. The government of Boca Verde was notoriously corrupt, almost in inverse proportion to the country's tiny size. Boca Verde was, in short, a whore, dispensing favors equally to tourists and terrorists. She offered a sanctuary for tax evaders, a breeding ground for covert intelligence. Boca Verde could boast of the hemisphere's earliest abortion and sex-change clinics, numbered bank accounts, death squads, and now, surveying everything, glittering Donald Trump-style casinos. All in all, a surreal, circus-scenery backdrop for the country's appalling poverty and violent land-reform struggles. Since Boca Verde had almost no exportable products or services, it chose instead to attract whatever foreign enterprises it could, dangling as bait almost nonexistent government regulations and a huge labor pool available at near-slave wages.

Here, in laissez-faire Boca Verde, the Cybernetic Temple found its perfect home.

Robbie stood apart from the crowd. He reached into his bag for a container of the Temple's shimmering powdered nutrient. He scooped up a handful and swallowed it in a ravenous gulp. He had eaten nothing but the powder in over three months now. It was a point of pride.

Outside the airstrip fencing, a jeep pulled up. A woman waved. Robbie raised his own arm tentatively. A strange sensation filled him. The vision of the distant woman excited him, heated him more than the tropical sun. He began trotting through the thick humidity, his clothes clinging like plastic. What was it he sensed about the woman? He didn't care that he was sweating. The woman was coming into focus now. Dark, trim, unsmiling. Robbie's breath came raw and labored. A rivulet of perspiration plopped into his eye, blurring the image of the woman and the jeep. He kept running. He reached the gate. He blinked and the woman came back into focus. Yes, now it was clear. She raised her arm once more in greeting, and Robbie saw distinctly what he had only intuited before—that the limb was prosthetic from the elbow down.

The vision and the heat merged in a sudden white light as Robbie collapsed beside the jeep.

•

When Robbie woke, long after midnight, there was no sign of the woman or the jeep. He did not know where he was, only that he had slept for a long time. His head felt like a block of concrete. He remembered fainting at the airport, and later, the half-formed sensations of being transported through the jungle, as if through a dream, to a gleaming complex. Shadowy figures, cool prosthetic fingers. Masks. Then, a sudden sharp stabbing at the crook of his arm. And dreams. Real dreams—

Robbie moved his legs slowly off the side of the bed. His head wobbled heavily as he pulled himself to a sitting position. Window blinds sliced the moonlight into pale diagonal shards across tiled walls. It was still dark, but tropical birds had already started to keen in anticipation of the dawn. What kind of drug had he been given? One not strong enough, evidently, to have him wake in the middle of the night. He was wearing some kind of paper gown. The room was very silent. Robbie knew instinctively that this was not a communal area. He had been looking forward to meeting the others, sharing their stories, their hopes. But there were no "others" here. He had awakened like a corpse in a morgue. Unexpectedly.

The tile was cool under his bare feet as he moved across the room and felt for the door. It was not locked. He stood at the end of a long corridor lined with laboratory windows. A faint fluorescent illumination from within the labs lent a phosphorlike glow to the floor and ceiling. As he approached the large door at the end of the corridor, he heard the faint whir of motors. Steady, relentless mechanical activity. The air was still and hot; sweat ran down his face. He lifted a hand to mop his brow and realized that his head had been shaved.

The sound continued. Distinct. Metronomic.

He focused his human eye on the door handle, watched his hand close on the mechanism. As he pulled it open, the beat of machine noise intensified. He felt all around him the cool pulse of the complex, the low throbbing frequencies almost beneath his current level of awareness. But there was a more specific, tangible sound he was approaching now; a nearby locus of hums, clicks, and whirs. He walked on a suspended pathway above a series of enclosures. He sensed that they were occupied, but their interiors were filled with shadows that his biological vision could not penetrate. One enclosure glowed, however. When he moved directly above it, he stopped. And looked down.

The thing resembled a child's tricycle, one elaborately outfitted with a web of control cables, cams, and hydraulics. At the center of the web, like a glistening spider, was the upper half of a human head. A miniaturized life-support system pumped fluids to the braincase. Dozens of spaghetti-thin strands of muscle tissue connected with nerves at the cranial base; they snapped like angry worms, maneuvering the control cable. Just under the staring eyes, where the lower head had been chopped away, a froth of mucus collected in a stalactite ridge. The entire mechanism lurched around violently, bumping monotonously against the walls of the pen. Almost deliberately. Almost as if it were trying to—

Robbie woke up. And screamed. It was an animal sound, but he didn't care. The brain cart, evidently excited by the sound, wheeled around even faster, driving itself against the concrete walls of the enclosure again and again and *again*—

They cut away his scream, of course. They cut away

everything they couldn't use. They dissected him neatly, retaining only the brain-box, the eye, and a fernlike structure of nerves. The flesh they threw to the jungle. And in the climate-controlled computer laboratory where nothing could rot, they replaced his blood with a colorless fluorocarbon analog. They inserted deep electrodes. When the visual cortex had been sufficiently mapped, they snipped off the eye and fed it to the birds. And Robbie sank deeper into the machine. Without the eye there was no up, no down, no day, no night. His consciousness was one with the machine, filled with glowing digital phantoms. He didn't understand the tasks that were demanded of him, didn't comprehend the ghostly display of winking digits that were now his only perceptual reality. But the machine could give pleasure and the machine could give pain, and in time he would learn.

And on the third day he stopped imagining that he was breathing, forgot that he had ever breathed at all.

IMMORTAL COILS

Diandra had no trouble entering Venus's house through the service gate. Her voiceprint had not been erased; there was no reason for it to have been. Everyone knew where she was; she had been on television and in all the papers. Most important, the voiceprint meant that Venus still trusted her. With her help, she could still get to Boca Verde, complete the mission she had started . . .

She wandered through the rooms, with their strange juxtapositions of Victoriana and postmodernism. She fondled an Art Deco vase in the hall. The fog was spreading in. The sound of the afternoon horn echoed plaintively across the bay. Diandra had never been in the house alone before, never unobserved. There had always been Venus. Venus and her piercing gaze. A gaze that followed her, controlled her, protected her. A gaze that she alternately feared and craved.

Now, she wanted Venus more than anything. Venus would know what to do. She would get her back on track, stabilize the gyroscope.

155

Diandra drifted through the house, observing details she had never really seen before. She experimented with the floor switches that were everywhere and controlled everything: doors, locks, lights, draperies, kitchen appliances, and surveillance equipment. She touched sculpted objects, some that Venus herself had made, before, with the guilty knowledge that she was experiencing sensations unvailable to Venus, even in her own house.

No, she shouldn't be thinking such things. It was the *old body*, creeping back. Perhaps her faith had been shaken. How much damage had Dr. Nagy done in his horrible clinic? Was she even worthy of Boca Verde now?

She climbed the stairs to the master bedchamber. Venus's pallet was as she remembered it: cool, symmetrical, pristine. She touched every surface, invisibly spreading the strange contagion that didn't affect her at all and would certainly not harm Venus. They were above such things. Diandra caressed the bedcover, the lamps, the dressing table and its surgical tray. She opened a drawer she had never opened before and found a smashed picture frame. Next to it, a photo of Venus as she had been before her accident. The arms in the photo had been torn off. Or, more precisely, chewed off.

Diandra slammed shut the drawer. She looked up and saw herself in the aluminum-framed mirror. She had changed. Regressed. Her hair had grown out, lost much of its silver coloration. She was puffy and worn . . . it was that animal food they had forced upon her. She couldn't let Venus see her like this—

Sounds from downstairs. Venus. But not alone.

Diandra hurried to Venus's closet of prosthetics and opened the door. Several pairs of limbs hung limply from armatures. They varied dramatically in size and design. Obviously, Venus had been expanding her wardrobe.

The voices were drawing nearer. Diandra's heart pounded. *Not like this. She can't see me like this.* She pulled the closet door shut and crouched in the shadows just as the bedroom door opened. Through a sliver crack, she was able to see Venus as she entered the room. She was followed by one of the Japanese businessmen Diandra remembered from the night Philip had brought her here. Diandra held her breath and pressed an eye against the pencil-thin opening.

"Let's have a look, shall we?" said Venus in her smoky contralto. As she floated past the narrow view-slit, Diandra could see that she wore a new set of arms; heavy, hydraulically pistoned, and vaguely paramilitary, they were more elaborate, powerful, and dexterous than any Diandra had seen before. *A gift. From a wealthy admirer.* She also wore a patch over her left eye.

Diandra nearly swooned as Venus approached the closet. She stopped just short of opening it—Diandra had forgotten the mirror on the side opposite. Mantislike, the sleek robotic arms reached up to remove the eye patch.

What lay beneath was not an eye at all, but reminded Diandra of the thing she had seen long ago in one of Robbie's dead sockets. But Venus's model was far more elaborate. And functioning. She heard the little camera motor whir, saw the iris dilate and contract.

"Yes . . . " Venus murmured. "Oh, yes . . . "

"I brought this along," said the Japanese businessman. "I thought you might like to keep it."

He reached into his pocket and withdrew a small Lucite cube into which Venus's former eye had been embedded. He set the little paperweight down in the surgical tray on her dressing table.

"That's very thoughtful of you," said Venus. "I'm sure it will appreciate in worth. As do *all* antiques. Now let's see the rest."

The mantis arms reached up to unfasten her loose-fitting garment. It fell to the floor. She was naked and

utterly unselfconscious about the Japanese businessman's presence. But it wasn't any wonder . . . there was
nothing to conceal any longer. The breasts were gone,
and in their place a pair of thin symmetrical scars,
angled down to the base of the rib cage. A perfect V, for
Venus. There were other scars on the abdomen as well,
but they were all perfectly balanced, controlled. *Cor-
rect from a design standpoint*, as Venus herself might
say.

"We have accomplished much," the Japanese businessman said. "The prosthetic designers were resistant
to your demands for the mechanical *look*—"

"If I wanted rubber skin, I could have gone to Disneyland. I wanted the structure articulated. People
objected to the Eiffel Tower once, for the same reasons
. . . in any event, they're not supposed to be human
arms. They're *more* than human."

"Indeed. And the artificial pancreas . . . it's a
masterpiece."

"Well, it took you long enough."

"There were many failures in Boca Verde. We didn't
dare approach you until the mechanics were perfected. We are so grateful for your continuing generos-
ity. We have learned so much about cybernetic grafts in
the process. The first biochip computers will be ready
soon, in no small part because of your help and encouragement. We have been honored to grant your requests. Without the participation of your disciples—"

"Oh, for God's sake, don't call them that. They were
just experimental animals wandering the streets. I
simply found them a home." She laughed. "You skin the
chinchillas . . . and I wear the coats."

"Yes. I think we understand each other, Venus."

"Well, I *do* hope your new computers are successful.
So many lives have been given in the cause, after all."

"Oh, we are expecting *complete* success."

Diandra sat numb in the closet. What did Venus
mean, *skin the chinchillas*?

A more or less standard series of acts ensued on the bedslab for the better part of an hour. The Japanese businessman seemed insatiably excited by the potentially viselike appliances as they manipulated his sex. Diandra watched him stroke a prosthesis, fondle it gently at the bionic juncture.

"Oh, yes . . . I did promise you something . . . *exotic*, didn't I? But these arms are all wrong! Let me slip into something a bit more . . . stimulating."

Venus strode back to the closet. And opened the door.

The mechanical eye dilated completely.

"Diandra—"

"I . . . I got away from him, Venus. I was strong, I didn't break—"

She rushed forward to embrace her cyborg goddess. "They injected me with things. Poisons. Diseases. The others got sick but I didn't. That's proof, isn't it? Proof that I can still be—"

Venus stiffened. Recoiled. "Diseases?" The Japanese businessman turned ashen. "Venus, the implants, the immunosuppressants, you can't tolerate—"

Venus's face went livid, then feverish. Beads of sweat gathered on her brow. Her skin began to pucker as the buboes and ulcerations began to appear. Her face contracted in pain, searing physical pain, the kind of sensation Diandra had always supposed that Venus had transcended.

Venus screamed. Ulcerations ripped along the nerve paths. The Japanese businessman came to her side, but she grabbed his wrist with her powerful arm. Diandra heard the bone crunch. *"Don't touch me!"* she cried, and hurled him against the wall. They were to be the last intelligible words she would utter at any volume. She swayed precariously, her face red, then purple, tongue and single eye bulging. The sounds she made now were animal sounds, the cries of a forest creature snared in a sophisticated trap. The bionic arms thrashed around crazily, and then, in a final, instinctive reflex, she began to use them to stop the pain the only way she could.

She started to tear off her flesh.

The first swipe of the mechanical claw took away half her face. No more nerve endings to bedevil her brain. She let the face-part fly in a wide arc, flecking the room in abstract patterns of blood and tissue. The second stroke ripped open the surgical scars on her torso. Blood shot in jets. Diandra could see bone. The Japanese businessman sank to his knees, tearing his hair. Venus's pincer-like hands rummaged through her viscera, and Diandra saw the plastic parts that had been woven into the abdominal cavity. Hot fluids poured onto the industrial carpeting. Spasms convulsed her. She gyrated wildly, a broken bloody toy, the one natural eye still jerking in its socket, the artificial one dilating and contracting, dilating and contracting. Her mouth opened in a silent scream that ended only when she pressed the hydraulic arms to her head like a pair of jackhammers. And used them.

Diandra watched the red plume of pulpy matter erupt from Venus's skull like the contents of a pulverized melon. For a moment, her brain was finally and totally free.

The ceiling drizzled back its catch as she collapsed upon the bed, a tangled heap of flesh and entrails and wriggling wires.

The Japanese businessman gave a strangulated cry and threw himself across the silent stinking mess that had once been Venus Tramhell. Diandra stood still, uncomprehending. Venus was dead. It was impossible, inconceivable. Venus was dead . . . and somehow *she* was responsible. The clinic. The contagion. If so, the Japanese businessman was doomed as well, though not to a fate so spectacular as the one she had just witnessed. To make doubly sure he would be put out of his pain, she stroked his head as she drifted past the tableau of death. His end would be slower, less showy, but soon he would know peace.

As Diandra left the room, she saw, or thought she saw him reach down into the twisted gore to retrieve something. And she saw, or thought she saw him hold it to his breast, peeling away the synthetic membrane that encased it. A tiny figure, vaguely human, mostly machine, a cyborg homunculus that struggled briefly and then fell still. Diandra thought she might have seen that.

She closed the door of the death chamber and used the hall bathroom to cleanse herself of the horror. There were fresh clothes in the closet, sunglasses and a turban. There was some money on the kitchen counter, crisp in a disinfected packet Venus would never use. Before she left she erased her voiceprint from the house security system. She wouldn't be coming back. Not in *this* life.

TRUE CONFESSIONS

The police offered to drive Gillian back to Marin, but she refused. *You've had a great shock*, they kept telling her. But she didn't feel any shock. She didn't feel anything. *You can't go on holding it in*, they told her. *Is there someone you can be with?*

No, she realized. There is no one I can be with.

She drove back to Marin. She decided to go to the beach house. She wanted to be by the ocean. By herself. She hardly spent any time there. But she was, after all, still married to Julian. She had a right to be there if she wanted to.

The car seemed to propel itself in a dreamlike fashion, as if she were traveling to a destination somewhere in her mind rather than to the rocky coastline north of San Francisco. Perhaps she was. Were there any other destinations, finally?

The police had questioned her for hours. She had told them about Venus, and Josh's suspicions. They checked it out and found that Tramhell had been out of

163

the country. Somewhere in Central America. That didn't rule out her involvement, but there was very little to go on. "He told you he was being threatened," Gillian told them in a calm voice. Over and over and over. They didn't care. They weren't embarrassed. They said they'd be talking to her husband as well. A waste of time, she could have told them. She'd been trying to talk to him for seventeen years. They said they'd be in touch. She'd left.

She arrived at the beach house at full moon and high tide. The lights were on. The security system, she supposed. But when she let herself in, she realized she was not alone.

"Julian . . . ?"

There was no answer, but she heard sounds. Strange, panting, animal noises. She went to the living room with its huge windows overlooking the surf. Julian was curled in a fetal position on the thick Berber carpeting in the center of the room. He didn't even look up or acknowledge her presence. He just crawled over to her and grabbed her by the ankles, sobbing. It was as if he had expected her to come.

"My God, Julian, what's wrong—?"

"The clinic . . . an accident . . . it's the end of everything, Gillian. I don't know whom to tell, how to start—"

So this was Julian Nagy, master media manipulator, talk-show masturbator, control freak, and husband. Helpless as a baby seal at her feet. Oblivious to whatever concerns *she* might have at the moment. Nothing new, of course . . . but whatever had happened this time must be serious. She had never seen him in such bad shape.

"He let her go . . . he killed himself and let her go . . . she's contagious—"

"Who are you talking about?"

"That girl, Diandra—"

"Why do you say she's contagious?"

Julian's breathing came slower, and he started to explain. He didn't have to explain much before Gillian pulled away. "My God, Julian, are you insane? Have you notified the authorities?"

"N-no . . . I was afraid . . ."

"Afraid?" She stared at him in disbelief. "Don't you understand the consequences—"

"I know what they'll do to *me*, if that's what you mean."

"Do you know what they'll do if you *don't* report this, and immediately?"

Julian laughed. "Either way, it's over. If there's a major epidemic, there'll be better publicity. You could write a book, Gillian. You and that boyfriend of yours with the rubber legs. Make a movie. Make a mint."

"What did you just say, Julian?"

"About your shack-up off Shattuck? Nothing, nothing. I just hope my outpatients haven't been hassling him too much . . ."

"Your outpatients—"

"I just thought I'd have a little fun. Throw a scare into him." His voice was thick with alcohol. "So I planted a few ideas in their little robot heads." He grabbed for the glass he had set on the carpet. It spilled, and he began picking up the ice cubes, rubbing them off.

"Julian, Josh is dead. They killed him."

Julian's heaves started almost immediately.

There wasn't time for Gillian to feel all the things she had to feel. She moved automatically to the bedroom and made two phone calls. One was to the police. The second was to New York, to Cherie. She left a message on her machine.

She left Julian puking in the beach house and she didn't look back. The police would know where to find him. She drove back to the old Victorian and went immediately to her office. She didn't have time to cry. Tomorrow she'd cry. Instead she took her typewriter out of its case and rolled in a sheet of paper. There were words to get out, if only a few tonight. The rest would follow. *She moved as if in a dream, and it was your dream*, she typed, *although at that point in time neither of you knew that the other existed, or mattered at all.*

This book is for you.

LAST RITES

Diandra moved among the Christmas shoppers unrecognized, brushing through the crowds on Union Square toward the place where she had begun her journey. There was a long line waiting to get into Croesus; as Philip had promised, they were charging admission, and the people were paying. She took her place in the queue, pretending to be one of them. The window displays were reflecting her obvious influence. There was a "Close Encounters" nativity scene with aliens for angels. Inside, it was promised, was the world's first robot Santa Claus. Your $5 admission charge could be applied to any purchase, the man at the revolving door informed her. No one seemed to object. They were hungry to worship at the Altar of Things.

Inside, Croesus had evolved beyond any past conception of retail marketing. The atmosphere was more like that of a club or disco. Banks of television screens were everywhere. Art Deco had been trimmed in flashing neon. She could discern the subliminal advertising messages that wafted through the air, products that seemed to whisper *touch me, hold me, buy me*. She ran her fingers across as many objects as she could, impregnating them with her own biogenetic gift. She made the grand tour of the store, from appliances to cosmetics, applying her hands in a lingering benediction. She stared at the slack, hypnotized faces of the customers and tried to imagine minds that actually believed that they controlled these objects, believed that they could control *her*. Temporary, contemptible beings, forged from fuck and grasping at straws. Soon they would know differently.

In the toy department she made a special point of tousling the beard of the android Santa, just the place where the children were sure to tug.

There. She had made her point, done her bit for biology. Now she was beyond all that. There was business to attend to. In Boca Verde.

She took the airport shuttle and a half hour later found herself at San Francisco International Airport. She went to the departure lounge to wait. Soon, she knew, an old friend from the Temple would signal her, make all the arrangements . . . tickets, passport, and the rest. Or perhaps even Venus—that display she put on in her bedroom was startling enough, but she knew that Venus could never *really* die. It was all just an elaborate stage trick, something to fool the Japanese businessman. No, Venus would be there in Boca Verde when she arrived; she was sure of it.

She waited quietly for a long, long time. And after a while, she realized, the departure lounge was completely deserted except for her. Of course. They understood the importance of her presence, the significance of her departure. It was only natural for them to show deference. There were human voices at a distance, loud, panicked; she filtered these out and waited for the mechanically amplified message that could be only for her. Finally, it came: *You must come with us*. She stood to face those who addressed her. A half-dozen figures, faceless behind airtight helmets, bodiless beneath aseptic white suits. *We repeat: you must come with us*.

Of course. Of course she would go with them. They were her escorts, after all. Cool beings to guide her. Their suits dazzled in the bright lights. A hundred mechanical eyes recorded her every move. She bowed curtly to acknowledge their mission, stretched out her arms to receive the sacrament. They rushed to surround her, cover her in a plastic shell. Diandra closed her eyes. They would be good to her, she knew, these creatures from beyond time and beyond the flesh. She gave herself up, then, relinquished her hold. She felt the sweet oblivion of ultimate transport by these emissaries from a new reality, of rescue, of surrender, of final communion with them all.

ELTING MEMORIAL LIBRARY
93 Main Street
New Paltz, New York 12561